Royals of Monrosa

Three princes, three royal romances!

Princes Edwin, Luis and Ivo couldn't be more different. But when their father, the king of Monrosa, announces his intent to abdicate the throne, they soon find themselves united in their royal duty.

And now they also have one more thing in common—their fight for true love! Because each of these princes is about to find themselves an unlikely princess. And they'll accept nothing less than governing their kingdom with their brides by their sides.

Discover Edwin's story in
Best Friend to Princess Bride
Available now!

And look out for Luis's and Ivo's stories
Coming soon!

Dear Reader,

Welcome to the first of the Royals of Monrosa trilogy. With each story I promise you an utterly compelling hero prince, a heroine you'll cheer on and the most beautiful locations for you to escape to.

I adore reading stories about best friends falling in love—they're always filled with emotionally complex story lines. Which is why I loved writing *Best Friend to Princess Bride*, as I got to experience intimately, word by written word, my gorgeous duo, Prince Edwin and Kara, fighting their romantic love for one another because of deeply held personal fears and the terror of losing the one thing that's vital in both of their lives—their friendship.

I hope you enjoy escaping to the blue Mediterranean skies of Monrosa Island and the wedding of the year!

Happy reading.

Katrina

Best Friend to Princess Bride

—

Katrina Cudmore

Recycling programs
for this product may
not exist in your area.

ISBN-13: 978-1-335-55620-2

Best Friend to Princess Bride

Copyright © 2020 by Katrina Cudmore

This edition published by arrangement with Harlequin Books S.A.

For questions and comments about the quality of this book,
please contact us at CustomerService@Harlequin.com.

Harlequin Enterprises ULC
22 Adelaide St. West, 40th Floor
Toronto, Ontario M5H 4E3, Canada
www.Harlequin.com

Printed in U.S.A.

A city-loving book addict, peony obsessive **Katrina Cudmore** lives in Cork, Ireland, with her husband, four active children and a very daft dog. A psychology graduate with an MSc in human resources, Katrina spent many years working in multinational companies and can't believe she is lucky enough now to have a job that involves daydreaming about love and handsome men! You can visit Katrina at katrinacudmore.com.

Books by Katrina Cudmore

Harlequin Romance

Romantic Getaways

Her First-Date Honeymoon

Swept into the Rich Man's World
The Best Man's Guarded Heart
Their Baby Surprise
Tempted by Her Greek Tycoon
Christmas with the Duke
Resisting the Italian Single Dad
Second Chance with the Best Man

Visit the Author Profile page
at Harlequin.com for more titles.

To Edith, thank you for your constant support, wisdom and friendship. Love, Katrina.

Praise for
Katrina Cudmore

"As it continued it drew you in more and more until the realization happened that you didn't want to put the book down. The story really does pull the reader into almost a black hole where nothing else exists. It's not a hot and heavy, but it is a couple of tissues, lots of heart strings and an emotional roller coaster of a ride. This is a book you will enjoy and love to share around."

—*Harlequin Junkie* on *Second Chance with the Best Man*

CHAPTER ONE

KARA DUFFY HIT the mud with a yelp. Cold muck and pebbles dashed her face. She sagged into the soft earth, every inch of her body aching.

Sucking footsteps, in a fight with the quagmire, approached behind her.

Could this day get any worse?

Not only was she, the poster girl for the charity's first ever fun mud run, going to be one of the last to cross the finishing line, but now one of her volunteer race marshals was having to come and rescue her. She needed to get up. Now. While she had some dignity left.

She pushed with all her might but her hands disappeared into the sogginess and her knees slipped and slid all over the place.

She gave a grunt and flipped over. Swallowing her pride.

But instead of a race marshal, three men, all in their thirties, all muscled and tanned, wearing top-to-toe tight-fitting black clothes, stood watching her. Two were considering her with professional concern, while the guy in the centre was trying desperately to hold back a laugh.

Prince Edwin of Monrosa and his royal protection officers, Domenico and Lucas.

Oh, what? Clamping her hands to her face, she gave a moan. Between her fingers she spotted Edwin grin. She giggled, relief surging through her, the weeks of disquiet over his lack of contact vanishing more swiftly than the grey March clouds scuttling across the sky behind him.

Lowering her hands, she grinned back at him, all of her work worries, her crabbiness over being so cold, her frustration at lagging so far behind in the field of competitors, disappearing in the face of his entrancing sorcerer's smile.

Edwin's hand reached down and he hoisted her out of the mud, an embarrassing squelching sound accompanying her escape.

With a barely detectable nod from Edwin, Domenico and Lucas moved away in the direction of the two event marshals who were standing at the stone piers at the top of the field that led out onto the return road to the event's tented village.

'You look exhausted.' Edwin paused, that smile still dancing on his lips. 'I'd offer to carry you but I don't want to be yelled at like the last time I pulled you up from a muddy field.'

Puzzled, she yanked her jacket down from where it had twisted around her waist and then she laughed. Of course! He was talking about the first time they had met. She had been seventeen and playing in a rugby cup game and had just been tackled by a prop forward built like a small garden shed. Winded, she had been trying to gather herself when she had been hoisted off the ground. She had expected a teammate but instead she had turned to find a dark-haired guy towering over her, the concern in his golden eyes stealing away her indignation. From the get-go, Edwin had appointed himself as her protector, her rock of good sense…and after Michael, her brother and Edwin's best friend, had died, despite her resistance he had become her mentor, her modern-day guardian angel.

Now, aching for a shower and hot chocolate at the finishing line, for once she was seriously tempted to take him up on his offer of assistance but of course didn't do so. 'You need to be careful with your back at your age.'

Edwin folded his arms. 'I'm only three years older than you.'

She gave him a sympathetic smile. 'Every year counts.'

He raised an eyebrow, his thumb flicking

across the tip of her nose. She shivered at the fierce concentration in his expression. Then, showing her his thumb, now covered in a smear of dirt, he said with his usual quiet humour, 'I'm guessing you don't need this particular memento of today's run,' pausing, he ran his eyes down the length of her mud-encrusted body, 'especially when you are already heading home with a small garden's worth.'

Kara blinked. And stepped away. His touch always made her feel peculiarly vulnerable. 'I need to get to the finishing line—the fund-raising team will be regretting persuading me to front up the campaign.' Rolling her eyes at Edwin's grin, she admitted, 'I can't believe I actually agreed to pose for those photos and marketing video of me dashing across the finishing line—I should have known they'd come back to haunt me.'

Turning away, she tackled the mud bath before her. He came and walked alongside her. 'So what has brought you here today? Isn't there some exotic beach or skiing trip missing you?' she asked.

'I decided to forgo my usual Sunday morning haunts to spend some time with you.' Taking hold of her hand again, to help her out of a deep hole she was failing to free herself from, he pulled her out and said gently, 'I know how much today means to you. I wanted to support you, especially as the race is named in Michael's honour.'

An ache for Michael rose up from the pit of her stomach and spread into her chest cavity like a smothering vapour until it wrapped around her heart, the loneliness of it physically hurting even a decade on. She swallowed down that ache to a place deep, deep inside of herself, balling her fists to create the energy to be upbeat and teasing with him. She lifted her head to meet his gaze. The man with the golden eyes and golden heart. 'I always appreciate your backing.' She gave him a wicked smile. 'As does the rest of my team—Kate and Triona were only lamenting earlier this morning the fact that we haven't seen a lot of you in the office in recent months.'

'Where are your team anyway? Why aren't you with them?' Edwin asked.

'I told them to go ahead, I was only holding them up. They needed to get to the finishing line early to thank everyone taking part in the run before they left. We had hoped for a bigger field today and need to persuade as many runners as possible to come back next year. If we can get the numbers right, this run will be a great way to raise funds and promote the work of the charity.'

Edwin's mouth tightened as once again he

had to yank her out of the mud. 'Somebody should have stayed with you.' Nodding towards her trainers—well, what was visible of them beneath the inches of mud—he added, 'And equally someone should have told you to wear something more practical.'

She gazed down at his feet and smirked. 'Like your special forces-issue boots, you mean? And don't go denying that you were trained by the Monrosa army—no one goes away, as you claim you did, on a three-month diplomatic tour and returns with biceps that would rival those of a heavyweight boxer.' As expected, Edwin gave his usual non-committal shrug, so she added, 'There was no need for anyone to stay with me for the race. I was doing fine until I came to the incline.'

He made a disbelieving sound. And her heart missed a beat as his gaze continued to hold hers with an unsettling intensity. Only now that he wasn't looking away did she realise just how rarely he fixed his eyes on her for any prolonged period. Disconcerted, she asked, 'Is something the matter?'

For a moment the faint lines around his eyes tensed, but then he turned and, still holding her hand, led her towards Domenico and Lucas, who were waiting for them alongside the course marshals. 'There's something I want to ask you. I need your help. But we can discuss it later.'

She allowed him to guide her out of the quagmire, wondering if this was the first time in all their years of knowing each other that he was asking for her help.

From the first moment that they had met he had helped her, and had shown no sign of stopping. There must have been a time when he had asked for her help...but for the life of her, she couldn't remember one. Yes, she had given him the support of friendship, shared his passion for old black and white movies and mountain trekking, the writing of Douglas Adams, but Edwin, so self-contained, so self-sufficient, so private, had never directly asked for her help. Even in those dark days and weeks after Michael's death, when grief had been chiselled into his face.

Now, as he led her out of the field, she inhaled a shaky breath, her chest tightening. How would she have coped if Edwin hadn't been there for her after her darling, her beloved, her troubled older brother had died? Her parents had fallen to pieces. They had idolised Michael as much as she had. The first family member to go to university. And Oxford at that. Their pain after his death had been unbearable to witness. Knowing Michael had taken his own life had been too cruel, too senseless, too wrapped in guilt and what-ifs. Kara had stood by and watched her dad try time and time again to reach her mum, searching for support, but her mum had shut him out, disappearing into a world of her own where there was no time or energy for anyone else. She had watched her dad plead, grow angry and eventually shut down. It had crushed Kara's idea of love and relationships to see all of that pain and helplessness wrought on her dad.

As their marriage fell apart and during their eventual divorce Kara had leant on Edwin, needing his support, his encouragement, his advice, his reproaches when she had self-destructively gone off the rails. She had somehow managed to sleepwalk her way through her A levels in the month after Michael had died and gone on to university. But there had been so many bumps along the road, including dropping out of university for a month, until Edwin had made her see sense.

And when she had finally taken her finger off the self-destruct button five years ago, for the first time accepting just how destructive her relationship with her ex-boyfriend Nick was, she had realised that there was one thing she wanted to achieve in life—to set up a charity focused on the mental health of young adults, particularly targeting the difficult years of transition after leaving school. Five years on, the charity had seven centres throughout the UK, ran transitioning and education programmes in conjunction with several universities and provided a twenty-four-hour helpline. But there was so much more that they needed to do. There were so many more young people and their families they needed to help, but the lack of resources was holding them back. The need to do more consumed her.

At the gateway out onto the road, they paused and Edwin shook hands with the marshals, who did a reasonable attempt at appearing to be nonchalant in meeting him, an actual, real-life prince.

When it was her turn to greet the men she pulled them into a group hug. 'Thanks for volunteering today. We couldn't hold fundraising events like this without the support of our volunteers.'

Both men held themselves as stiff as a board and when she released them they eyed her as though they were worried for her sanity and their own safety.

'Kara's the founder and chairperson of Young Adults Together,' Edwin explained with amusement.

Both men relaxed.

One of them, heavily built with long hair and

a skull nose piercing, said in a pronounced Cornish accent, 'This morning I was up before dark to come and do my bit.' Reddening, he cleared his throat, rolled his shoulders, and continued, 'My daughter…went through a bad patch last year.'

Kara swallowed at the confusion and fear in his voice. He cleared his throat noisily. 'Your counsellors gave us a lifeline when we didn't know where to turn.'

Kara pulled him into another hug. This time he wrapped his arms around her.

After she had extracted a pledge from both men that they would continue to volunteer for the charity, she hobbled as quickly as she could alongside Edwin on the internal estate road that led back to the tented village which had been erected adjacent to Fairfield House, thanks to the generosity of Lady Fairfield, who, along with Edwin, was a patron of the charity.

Domenico went ahead of them, while Lucas stayed a distance behind.

After graduating, Edwin had worked in the City of London for four years before returning to Monrosa to act as global ambassador for its financial sector. His job brought him to London on a regular basis but for the past month he had remained in Monrosa and his contact with Kara had mainly consisted of the occasional rushed text. 'I haven't heard from you recently—have you been busy?'

Beside her Edwin came to a stop. Kara's heart did a somersault at how troubled he suddenly seemed.

'You're limping.'

Giddy relief ran through her. For a moment she had thought something was seriously wrong. She reached down and rubbed the back of her thigh. 'I think I pulled something.'

Crouching down beside her, Edwin said, 'Show me where exactly.'

Kara pointed to the mid-centre of her thigh with her index finger. 'There.'

His hand touched her mud-strewn thigh, his warm fingers softly tracing over the skin beneath her running shorts. Every muscle in her body tensed as she resisted the temptation to yelp, giggle, move away.

'You've pulled your hamstring. We need to get you back to the finishing line quickly so that you can ice and elevate it.'

His gaze moved up to gauge her reaction.

'Why are you here, Edwin?'

Instead of answering her question he stood and said, 'I'll carry you to the finishing line.'

Kara laughed but she soon stopped. He was being serious. 'I'm fine. And anyway, I have to make my own way there—my sponsorship depends upon it.'

'How much is your sponsorship worth?'

'Close to two thousand pounds.'

For long seconds he held her gaze and Kara's heart gave a little kick. She should look away, make some quip, but now that he was here she realised just how acutely she had missed him over the past month.

'I'll match your sponsorship.' And then, with one of those utterly charming smiles of his, where she felt as if she was the centre of his world, he added softly, 'Now, please let me carry you. You're injured.'

For a nanosecond she actually contemplated his offer. But then good sense kicked in and she walked away. 'I've only pulled my hamstring. And how would it look to all of the other participants if the event organiser not only finished last but also had to be carried over the finishing line? By you of all people.' A safe distance away from him, she turned back. 'You know the media would have a field day if you're spotted carrying me. When are they ever going to accept that we're only friends?'

Edwin came alongside her. 'My father and mother had an arranged marriage. They started off as friends.'

Why was he telling her this? And she couldn't

remember the last time he had spoken about his mother, who had died when he was a teenager.

Before she got the opportunity to ask him what was going on, his arm wrapped around her waist and she almost jumped out of her skin. They weren't the touchy-feely variety of friends.

'Your limp is getting worse. If you refuse this help then I'm going to instruct Lucas to carry you to the finishing line.'

Preferring the unsettling effect of being so close to Edwin over the ignominy of being carried by Lucas, who frankly scared her a little with his silent-killer type intensity, she allowed him to support her, but didn't lean as much into his strength as she really needed to.

'My father still misses my mother. They were a good team. Maybe practical marriages are the answer.'

Okay, this conversation was getting odder and odder. 'Answer to what?'

Nodding in the direction of the tented village, which had just come into view, rather than answer her question Edwin asked, 'How much will the mud run raise for the charity?'

Why hadn't he answered her question? 'Close to twenty thousand pounds, which will secure counselling services in Southampton for the first three months of next year.'

'You know I'm happy to provide more funding.'

This was an ongoing argument between them. 'Yes, and I appreciate your offer. But I don't want you funding the charity…there are so many others you support. I want Young Adults Together to be funded by the local communities—it builds a better understanding and ownership of the issues involved, along with helping to destigmatise mental health issues.'

He gazed at her with a fondness that burnt a hole right through her heart. 'I'm very proud of you, do you know that?'

Kara shrugged, rolled her eyes, trying not to let her delight, but also alarm, show. When he spoke to her like that, it made her feel totally exposed and fearful as to what her life would be like if he wasn't part of it.

Leaving the dual carriageway and following the main artery into Brighton, a sea of red brake lights appearing ahead of him, Edwin slowed and eventually brought his SUV to a stop.

Beside him, Kara sighed heavily. 'There are roadworks ahead. They've been causing traffic chaos for the past week.' Turning to glance at the car directly behind them, she added, 'There really was no need for you to drive me all the way home to Brighton. I feel so guilty Domenico and Lucas are having to drive my car back for me.'

Studying his protection officers in his rear-view mirror, Edwin grinned at their scowls and at how they were taking up every spare inch of space in the front of Kara's tiny car that made him wince each time he saw it, not just because of its canary-yellow bodywork but also because he doubted it would offer her much protection in an accident. She refused to trade it in on environmental grounds. 'I didn't want you driving when you should be resting your leg.'

Kara let out an impatient huff and shifted the icepack he had earlier taken out of the first-aid kit in the boot.

'It's a pulled hamstring and not even a seriously pulled one at that. It's fine,' Kara protested, her nose wrinkling with annoyance, the freckles on her cheeks she usually covered with make-up standing clear and proud.

'I like you without make-up and your hair like that. It reminds me of how you looked when we first met.' He hadn't meant to go out onto the rugby field that day, but seeing her brilliantly dodge endless tackles through intelligent and courageous play the length of the pitch, only to be thwarted at the try line, he had roared in frustration, and then, seeing her inert on the ground, her face buried in the earth, her limbs sprawled, he had raced onto the pitch, the need to get to her, to protect her all-consuming. And to this day that need to protect her was still there. A need that had solidified after Michael's death. Seeing her despair, her loneliness as her family fell apart, he had vowed to protect her, to always support her.

Michael's funeral had been a nightmare. Kara's parents, who were both deeply private individuals, had resented the media attention Edwin's presence had attracted and, already wracked with guilt over whether he could have done more to help his friend, he had listened to Kara say quietly and with a heartbreaking dignity in her eulogy that she had lost her first ever best friend, her inspiration, and he had silently pledged he would always be there for the little sister Michael had adored.

At times, he had struggled. Her pain had mirrored his own grief—not only for the loss of his best friend, but also from losing his mother and the unearthed memories and feelings he wanted to keep buried. But as they had got to know each other over the years their relationship had moved to one of firm friendship, and Kara, with her straight talking and dry sense of humour, gave him balance and perspective and a sense of normality he could so easily lose in a life where people were always way too eager to please him.

Was he about to put their entire relationship

in jeopardy? Was he about to compromise the trust between them? Frustration towards his father and fear for the future had him wanting to open the car door and break into a run.

Oblivious to the bombshell he was about to deliver to her, Kara gave him a horrified look, flipped down her sunshade and stared at her reflection in the mirror. 'Are you kidding me? I can't believe I forgot my make-up bag this morning. And as for my hair...' She paused and lifted her long, honey-blonde curls with a grimace. 'Remind me to arrange for there to be a few hair straighteners in the women's changing rooms next year.' She gave a shiver and flipped the sunshade back up. 'I look terrible. I need a serious dose of sunshine—I look like I've spent ten years locked away indoors.'

Admittedly there was the hint of dark circles on the delicate pale skin beneath the sweeping brush of her long eyelashes, but the brilliance of her crystal-blue eyes hid that tiredness from all but the keenest of observers. 'I take it you are still working insane hours.'

Ignoring his comment, she flicked the radio to another station and then another, not settling until she found one playing jazz. She knew he hated jazz.

Ahead there was still no movement in the traffic. Flicking the radio off, he said, 'I saw you hobbling around the refreshment marquee when you were chatting to the runners—my guess is that your leg is a lot more painful than you're letting on.'

She rolled her eyes but then turned in her seat and regarded him with an appreciation that always caught him right in the gut. She followed it with the double whammy of her wide smile that always exploded like a firework in his heart, radiating a lightness inside him that always threatened the protective cloak of royal circumspection he had been taught to adopt from an early age.

'Thanks for coming in to say hello. The runners were thrilled to see you. I think you've guaranteed the success of next year's run. We were inundated with runners asking if they could sign up,' she said.

'I'm sure their interest in participating next year is down to how well the event was organised today and nothing to do with me.'

'Oh, please. You know the huge crowd waiting at the finishing line were there for a reason. And it certainly wasn't to cheer me on. Apparently there was a stampede back to the finishing line once word got around that you were spotted starting the race late—from our female runners in particular.' Nodding in the direction of the car behind them, she added with a grin,

'You and the guys did look rather fetching in your tight running gear.'

When was the traffic going to move again? He had things he needed to say to her. Things that were tying his stomach in knots. He had spent the last couple of weeks with a team of lawyers trying not to be in the position he was now in. What he had to ask of her was huge and unfair. He didn't want to drag her into this mess that wasn't of her making. But there was no one else he could trust. Dryly he responded to her teasing, 'I'm glad we proved to be of some use.' Then, unable to resist teasing her back, he added, 'I reckon it might be safer if you stick to the sidelines next year, though.'

'No way! I mightn't be special-services fit like you but I can hold my own. Trust me, I've learned my lesson and I'll pace myself much better next year.' She gave him a hopeful smile. 'It would be great if you could take part again. I can get Triona to contact your office with the date and hopefully if you are free they'll be able to schedule it into your diary.'

He arched his neck. Being stuck in a traffic jam was not the ideal place for this conversation but he couldn't go on pretending his life hadn't been turned upside down any longer. 'I'm not sure I'll be in a position to take part next year.'

For a moment she frowned but then she visibly paled. Her hand shot out to touch his arm. 'You're not ill, are you? Is that why you haven't been in touch recently?'

Her immediate concern for him only ratcheted up his guilt. He had sworn he would protect Michael's little sister, and here he was, asking her to step into the unrelenting scrutiny of the entire world.

He and Michael, who had both been students at Oxford, had met through the aikido club. As it had turned out, both of them were in Mansfield College studying Politics, Philosophy and Economics, Edwin a year ahead of Michael. On several occasions, Michael had brought him to his family home in London, claiming he needed to be exposed to the reality of how others lived. In London, Michael had taken him to the homeless charity where he had volunteered when in sixth form, and to his local aikido club, where he heard about their programmes to encourage teenagers into sport and away from knife crime. And Kara had tagged along, listening attentively to Michael's opinions, smiling when Edwin and Michael disagreed over some issue. She had visited Michael in Oxford and had gone to parties with them, the only person to ever persuade Michael out onto the dance floor. Kara had idolised Michael and their parents had worshipped him. Edwin used to tease him over it, Michael always shrugging it off until one evening during his second year in Oxford, when they were both at a house party. Michael was drunk and fell and spilt a drink all over someone's laptop. The owner screamed at Michael. Michael just stood there staring at the girl as she ranted at him, not reacting, looking as though nothing was registering with him. And then he disappeared out of the house. Edwin followed him, unsettled by the blankness in Michael's expression.

Edwin finally found him in the gardens of Mansfield. He almost backed away when he realised Michael was crying. Edwin had been brought up to hide his emotions. He didn't know how to cope with someone else's. But he went and sat down next to Michael. And they must have sat in silence for at least twenty minutes before Michael admitted just how much he was struggling to fit in at Oxford, how apart he felt from student life, his constant anxiety, how he feared disappointing his family, how riddled his mind was with dark, negative thoughts. Edwin listened, tried to help, but he was way out of his depth and ill-equipped to deal with Michael's despair. He encouraged Michael to reach out to the support services in the university and offered to pay if Michael would prefer to go to see someone privately.

And after a lot of resistance, they ended the

night hugging, Michael promising to contact the university health services. But in the weeks that followed, Michael shut Edwin down whenever he asked how he was doing. He disappeared off campus or spent days locked away in his room, claiming he was studying and didn't want to be disturbed.

In the run-up to their end-of-year exams, Edwin spoke to the college authorities about his concern over Michael's welfare. Michael learned of his intervention and went ballistic, refusing to speak to him again. Edwin called Michael's parents one night, a call he had agonised over for days, not wanting to betray Michael's privacy or to panic his parents unduly. He spoke to Michael's dad, who responded with disbelieving bewilderment. He told Edwin that, while he appreciated his concern, he was certain he was wrong. For hadn't Michael only told them the previous weekend just how much he was enjoying university life and was looking forward to staying with Edwin in Monrosa over the summer?

Michael failed his second-year exams. The day after he learnt his results he caught a train to the south coast and took an overdose on the beach that night. Early the following morning he was found by a local man.

His parents were away on holiday. Kara was the first to be told.

Kara called Edwin in Monrosa, sobbing and, despite several attempts, unable to tell him what was the matter. It was their neighbour who quietly whispered those words of horror down the phone to him.

Within an hour he was on his way to London. Once there, he held Kara, his heart torn in two by her mute, violent shivering, all the memories of holding his youngest brother, Ivo, the morning of their mother's funeral haunting him, reminding him how Ivo too had shuddered with grief, his fragile bones rattling in his arms.

When his mother had died he had thought that the grief of losing her would simply be about the gut-aching sadness and disbelief—he had never anticipated the ugly swamp of consequences that kept flowing back into his family's lives and swallowing them whole. Their father's angry, authoritarian way of trying to be an effective single parent, Luis's rebellion, which had seen him constantly in trouble with authority, Ivo's avoidance of them all, his own deliberate distance.

Loving someone too much destroyed you.

And in the aftermath of Michael's death, all those emotions had been stirred up again and he had relived the agony of losing someone.

Through the shock and grief and guilt he had
somehow managed to care for and support Kara,
encouraging her to continue with her studies,
and to accept her university place, and as time
passed they had become close friends, their relationship managing to survive media intrusion
and endless arguments when Kara was testing
every boundary possible, crying out for attention.

And now he was about to ask her a question
that could blow apart the one friendship that
kept him sane.

He lowered his window. Drops of drizzle immediately speckled the interior of the car door
but he needed some air to clear his brain. On a
deep inhale he admitted, 'I might not be able
to take part in the race next year because by
then I might have succeeded to the throne of
Monrosa.'

For long moments Kara stared at him, grap-
pling for words. 'When did this happen?'

'My father has decided to abdicate.'

'And you're next in line.' Looking away, she
stared at the still stationary traffic and said dis-
tractedly, 'There must have been an accident
ahead.' Then, her gaze shifting back to him, she
shook her head. 'Wow. I didn't see that coming.
But you don't seem very excited. I thought suc-
ceeding was what you always wanted.'

In the distance a siren sounded, and it came closer and closer until a police car passed them on the hard shoulder. He winced at the piercing sound. 'Both the royal court and the public will be slow to accept this change in ruler, especially when I push through my reforms to halt the ever-increasing mass tourism to allow for more sustainable development on the island to protect the environment.'

For long seconds Kara studied him, her ability to get to the core of a problem apparent in the reckoning in her eyes. 'You need to sell your vision of the Monrosa you want to rule. Ground that vision in what you already stand for—prosperity for all while protecting both the environment and the vulnerable in society. Look at all the changes you've already made by persuading your father to reform environmental policy. And there are all your ideas on housing and healthcare reform. I know you'll rule with loyalty and compassion while ensuring Monrosa continues to thrive. And the people will come to see and appreciate that too, with time.'

He could not help but laugh at the passion in Kara's voice. 'Maybe I should employ you as my press officer.' Then, sobering at the thought of the momentous battles he would have in the future, he added, 'Those environmental reforms aren't enough—they are only the start. Changing the mind-sets of the people, especially those heavily invested in the tourism industry, will not be easy. Environmentally responsible tourism and the attraction of other service industries, especially the financial-services sector, has to be the way forward for Monrosa's economy.' He let out a heavy sigh, '*Dio!* We have ruined long stretches of the coastline already with overdevelopment. My father sees no issue with it, but it's unsustainable. I need to succeed to the throne to stop any further development. We need to set in place a twenty-year plan for keeping the economy viable whilst protecting the unique environment of Monrosa.' His mother had been a passionate campaigner for protecting Monrosa's unique microclimates and biodiversity, and Edwin was determined to put the protection of the environment centre stage during his reign.

Kara nodded. 'And you will succeed in putting that plan in place. I know you will.' Then, pausing to bite her lip, she added, 'I'm guessing I'll get to see even less of you once you are crowned. Is that why you haven't been in contact recently?'

'I've spent the past month trying to persuade my father to stay in the role. I'm not convinced he's abdicating for the right reasons.' Seeing Kara's quizzical look, he added, 'He believes it's time for fresh ideas and a new energy in the role.' Then, rubbing his hand over his jaw, Edwin admitted, 'My father also says that he wants to ensure he has grandchildren before he's too old to enjoy them.'

'What has your father abdicating got to do with him becoming a grandfather?'

Edwin inhaled a deep breath. 'My father quietly passed a new piece of legislation last year on succession in Monrosa. From now on, only a married individual can be sovereign.'

Kara tilted her head and gave a small exhale of puzzlement. 'What does that mean?'

Doubt and misgivings and fear stirred like a trinity of foreboding inside him. He wasn't into relationships, never mind marriage—there was too much expectation around the need for love and intimacy. And Edwin's heart was too closed to ever risk loving another person again. Was he really prepared to enter into the minefield of marriage because it was his duty to do so? That question was easily answered. His destiny was to be crowned Sovereign Prince. He owed it to his country, his family, his people. 'I have to marry or my aunt, my father's sister, Princess Maria, will succeed to the throne.'

Kara laid her head against the headrest and let out a heavy, disbelieving breath. 'You're getting married.' She looked away, out to the grey and abandoned-looking industrial estate on the opposite side of the road, her hair obscuring her face.

'That's why I'm here today, to tell you. There's something I need...'

Before he could say anything more Kara twisted back to him, shifting in her seat and giving him a smile that didn't reach her eyes. 'Well, I suppose congratulations are in order. Who's the lucky woman and when is it all going to happen?' Then with a brief laugh she added, 'No wonder you disappeared off the face of the earth for the past month. I thought you were caught up with work and royal duty, not planning the wedding of the year.'

'My father intends on announcing his abdication next Thursday. The coronation date of the next monarch is already arranged—it will take place on the first of June.'

'So you have to be married by then?' Not waiting for him to respond, Kara said, 'That's just over two months away. So who are you going to marry? Are you already engaged? Is the wedding date set?'

Another police car, siren blaring, passed on their inside. He waited for the sound to fade out before he said, 'Earlier I said I needed your help...'

Kara waited for him to continue. After years

of embracing bachelorhood, his brain was still struggling to keep up with the new reality his father had decided to foist on him.

Folding her arms, Kara said, 'Please don't tell me you want me to be your best woman or something like that. I'm sure Luis can manage to behave himself for once and deliver a fitting best man's speech. And if not, I'm sure Ivo could be persuaded. Eventually.'

Did she really think he would become engaged to someone else without forewarning her or at least telling her he was heading in that direction? 'No! Not that. What I want to ask you...' he paused, gave her an uneasy smile that did nothing to diminish her unimpressed scowl '... I want to ask you to marry me. I want you to be my wife.'

CHAPTER TWO

HAD SHE BANGED her head earlier, when she had fallen? She could have sworn Edwin had just asked her to marry him. Was she suffering severe confusion as a result of concussion?

A loud rapping on Edwin's window made them both jump. Domenico was standing there and gesturing ahead, pointing out that the traffic in front had moved on and now Edwin was holding things up.

Nodding, Edwin pulled away.

Kara studied him, and it felt as though she was truly seeing him for the first time in ages. Was this man—this prince, this soon-to-be sovereign—actually asking her to marry him? His concentration was on the road ahead, his mouth pulled into a tight line, a hint of colour in his high cheekbones.

She laughed and said, 'Nice joke, Edwin. Now, why don't you tell me who you're really going to marry?'

He darted a look in her direction, the cleft in his jaw more pronounced than usual. He was seriously hacked off. 'I wouldn't joke about asking you to marry me. Surely you know that?'

Yes, she did. Edwin wasn't cruel. He was honourable and selfless. But right now she was grasping at straws in a bid to try to make sense of this conversation.

'I'm serious, Kara. I'd like you to be my wife.'

'Wow. I never thought I'd be so lucky as to be proposed to somewhere as romantic as a gridlocked dual carriageway on a gloomy Sunday in March.'

'I promise you a nice honeymoon.'

Kara laughed. 'Have you completely lost your mind?'

'Remember the time you rang me in the middle of the night and said that if we both got to thirty and were still single then we should marry?'

Oh, God, she'd hoped he had forgotten about that.

'I was tipsy and emotional at a friend's wedding. I wasn't being serious. I'm not interested in marrying.' In the immediate years after witnessing her parents' marriage implode, she had steered well clear of any relationship that could end so painfully. So she had dated guys who she knew wouldn't hang around, and for a while that had suited her fine. But after graduating, with her family home sold and living alone in Brighton because of work, she had craved stability and closeness. She had thought Nick was the answer to her embarrassing hunger for intimacy and she had embraced their relationship like someone famished. But his early attentiveness had slowly morphed into claustrophobic controlling behaviour and had once and for all firmly convinced her a single life was preferable to the minefield of relationships and the hurt they spawned. Now, folding her arms, she pointed out, 'And anyway, I'm not thirty yet.'

'In six months you are.'

'Thanks for the reminder.' She had a good life, one that was hard fought for after years of uncertainty and grief—supportive friends, a career that gave her meaning, and, most important of all, an uncomplicated personal life that left her free to focus on work, and work alone. Why, then, did hurtling towards thirty leave her with a nagging sense of unease? Was it the frustration of knowing there was an ever-increasing demand for the charity's services both in the United Kingdom and abroad? She desperately wanted to do more. There was so much work to be done in addressing mental-health issues and educating both young people and those who supported them about dealing with matters before they got out of control. Was it this constant feeling of not doing enough that left her unsettled as she faced her thirtieth birthday?

At a pedestrian crossing on a suburban street, Edwin stopped to allow a young man pushing a pram and holding hands with a little girl to cross the road. Kara shared sporadic phone conversations with her parents and usually they were short and revolved around the weather, but a few months ago her mum had surprised her when she asked her what she thought Michael would have been doing by now? Would he have had a career in political activism, as he had dreamed? Would he have been married? Had children? And after the call, she had sat in the silence of her apartment and wondered once again if she could have prevented Michael from dying.

Her gaze shifted to Edwin. He had been her constant, her steadying influence over the past decade. His marriage proposal was not only insane but it was also sending a tidal wave of uncertainty into her life when she had thought she had finally got a handle on it. 'There must be a long line of more suitable women out there— shouldn't you be trying to forge some strategic alliance, or whatever it is you royals do?'

Edwin waited until he had pulled into her street and found a parking space before he answered. 'I need to marry someone I can trust.'

Killing the engine, he unbuckled his seat-belt and turned and regarded her with that regal look of his that spoke of pride and honour. 'And there's no one I trust more in life than you.'

Her heart catching at the sincerity of his voice, she unbuckled her own belt. 'That's not exactly a solid basis for a marriage, though, is it? I'm sure you trust Domenico and Lucas but you're not about to marry one of them.'

Edwin eyed her with a raised eyebrow. 'I can't. They're both married. And there isn't time for them to get divorced. I need to announce my engagement before Thursday; my father is insistent on announcing his abdication then.'

Domenico came alongside the car. Edwin nodded that they were ready to go into Kara's flat. Reaching for the handle of his door, Edwin added, 'I reckon trust is the most important part of any marriage. At least we have that.'

Should she tell him that she didn't want him to come inside? She needed some time and space to make sense of his bombshell proposal. But what was there to think about? There was no way she could marry Edwin.

Inside her basement apartment, she placed her gym bag in the tiny utility room off the kitchen and went and filled her kettle.

Turning to Edwin, she said with a sigh, 'I'm a working-class girl—I have no idea how to be a princess. Even saying the word "princess" feels ridiculous. Me, a princess? No way.'

'The title would be Her Serene Highness, Princess of Monrosa,' Edwin said, removing his black padded jacket and hanging it on her bulging coat rack.

'See—I didn't even know what the correct title would be.'

He shifted the stool he always sat on away from the kitchen counter to allow for the extra-long length of his legs. Sitting, he shrugged. 'You're not expected to know royal protocol. None of that is of importance. What is important is that I have a wife I can trust, a wife who understands that what we'll have is a working marriage. I know how keen you are for the charity to be able to help more people—you could use your status to achieve that.' Rubbing the back of his neck, he said, 'I know what it is I'm asking of you, Kara, and I'm not asking it of you lightly. I have spent the past week agonising over whether to do so, but I think we can make it work. Neither of us is looking for romance… at least that's what you've always claimed.'

His last sentence sounded like a challenge. As though he was testing her constant refrain over the years that marriage was not for her. 'It isn't just a love marriage I'm not interested in, Edwin. It's all types of marriage.' Filling the teapot with boiling water, she added, 'I know this might sound a little rich coming from me, given my outlook on love, but *you* shouldn't discount love—you've never given it a chance. At least I gave it a go. You've always ended relationships way too early.'

Edwin made a grumbling sound and, leaning heavily against the counter, sent a teaspoon clattering across the marble surface. 'I'm happy being single.'

Placing four teacups on the counter, Kara stepped back, folded her arms and raised an eyebrow.

Edwin's gaze narrowed. 'What?'

Kara continued to hold his stare.

'Look, I just like to be careful who I trust. You've done pretty much the same since Nick,' he argued.

'Agreed, but then I'm not the one who now needs to marry. Maybe if you had been more open to those few women you actually dated over the years, willing to trust them, then you wouldn't have to resort to asking your friend to marry you.'

Edwin stood and, pacing the tiny floor space of her kitchen, raised his hand in exasperation. 'Like how I trusted Salma Rosucci?'

Kara winced. 'I'll admit it was unfortunate that Salma told the paparazzi you were holidaying together in Sardinia.' Biting back a smile, she added, 'On the positive side, the photos they took of you sunbathing cheered up millions of women across Europe.'

Edwin scowled. Then, walking towards her, he placed a hand on the countertop next to her and asked with quiet pride, 'Would marrying me be that bad?'

For a moment something deep inside her wanted to say no, that marrying him would be... would be okay. Better than okay, in fact. She would get to spend her days with him. Would that be such a bad thing? But then logic kicked in. Picking up the teapot, she poured tea into all four cups. 'The media are going to go crazy.'

'Let them. They'll soon come to recognise what an incredible person you are.'

'They'll eat me alive first. I can see the headlines—*"Prince Edwin to Marry Builder's Daughter."* Or how about, *"Why is Kara Duffy Marrying Billionaire Prince Edwin?"* And what will your family say?'

'Luis and Ivo don't care about what I do— they're too busy leading their own lives.'

'And what about your father?'

'He doesn't have the right to an opinion. He may have forced my hand on marriage but he has no say in who I marry.'

Kara buried her head in her hands. 'In other

words, he's not going to be happy when he finds out you've chosen me.' At best Kara would have said his father was indifferent to her whenever she visited the palace, and there were certainly times when he seemed to think she was an annoying creature sent to test his patience. 'I know he still blames me for that time I went out racing with you both and cost you the competition because I was so seasick we had to go back to the marina.'

'As I've said before, don't take it personally— my father is cantankerous with everyone. Including his own children.'

'But he rarely speaks to me and the last time I visited the palace he called me Salma...not only does he not know my name but he also mistakes me for one of your ex-girlfriends. Does he know you want to marry me?'

'No.'

A thought snaked its way into her brain. 'Asking me to marry you wouldn't be your way of getting back at your father, would it?'

Unbelievably he grinned at that. 'I hadn't thought of it that way, but it could be an added bonus.'

Shaking her head at the constant tension that existed between Edwin and his father, she pushed a cup along the counter towards him. 'I'd almost be tempted to say yes, just to witness first-hand how you and your father manage the succession; you'll drive each other insane with your alpha-male jostling.'

She carried the other two cups to the front door.

Edwin followed her. 'Alpha-male jostling. Where the hell did you get that idea from?'

She laughed at his indignation. 'It's a constant battle between you two—can't you see that? You and your father are too alike—that's why you clash. You both always want to be in control, the decision maker, the leader.'

He gave her a disbelieving look. 'No, we clash because my father is stubborn and work obsessed.' Indicating the teacups, he added, 'You know, you really don't need to give tea to Domenico and Lucas.'

'So you pointed out the last time you visited, and the time before that. And several times before that too. I hate the thought of them sitting out there in the cold with nothing to drink.'

Unlatching the door, instead of standing aside to allow her to go outside, Edwin took the cups from her. 'I'll bring them out—you should be resting. And making tea for the protection team will be a definite no when you're a princess.'

'I hate to point out the obvious, but I haven't agreed to be a princess.'

He gave her a grin. 'Not yet. But you will.'

He stepped outside. She called out, 'And you think your father's stubborn,' before going into the sitting room, where she turned on some table lamps against the fading light of the day and then lit the fire before going back into the kitchen to fetch their teacups.

Back in the hallway, she met Edwin on his way back in and she gestured for him to follow her into the sitting room.

She took a seat on the occasional chair beside the fire. Edwin carried a low stool from beneath the window and placed it before her. She lifted her leg onto the stool, wincing at the tightness that gripped her thigh.

Edwin sat on the sofa facing the fire, tucking a leg under himself, an arm running along the back of the navy sofa that was too small for his bulk. The flames from the fire cast shadows on his face. And then his eyes met hers. Silently he waited for her answer.

'I can't marry you, Edwin.'

'Why?'

'Where do I start? My background. What if something goes wrong? I like being your friend. I don't want to lose that.'

He shifted forward in his seat, his eyes holding hers all the time. 'I promise never to hurt you.'

Edwin always kept his word, but what if he

couldn't do so in this instance? Sometimes, despite their best intentions, people hurt each other. Not in a deliberate way like Nick, but purely due to human fragility. Look at what had happened between her parents. At first Kara had stood on the sidelines, bewildered and frightened, watching their pain and guilt and dismay over losing Michael destroy their love for one another. They had once loved each other. She was certain of that. But just not enough to counter the tsunami of grief losing Michael had caused. Her dad had looked to her mum for support, but she had pushed him away. Day after day she had watched her mum turn her back on her dad, grow more remote and uninterested in everything, while her dad had become more desperate, constantly trying to get through to her, to make things okay. Eventually, and not surprisingly, her dad had stopped trying, and had become bitter and defensive. It was the speed of it all that still astounded her: within weeks their family life had been stripped away and they were behaving no differently to three strangers living under one roof.

'What are you most scared of?'

She stared into the fire, considering his question, and then studied her ring-free fingers. Nick had given her a ring to mark their anniversary of dating for a year. He used to sulk when she

didn't wear it. She hadn't worn a ring for years.
The thought of even doing so now made her
wince.

She understood why it was so important to
Edwin to marry and she hated not being in the
position to help him on this one occasion that
he had asked for her support, so, despite the
tightness in her throat, the wave of vulnerability rolling through her, no matter how sickening it was to have to rake up old memories, the
least he deserved was her honesty. 'I'm scared
of feeling suffocated, losing myself in a relationship, even in a marriage of convenience.'

'I'm not following.'

She swallowed, the ability to talk suddenly
vanishing. 'After Michael…well, you know how
crazy my life got for a while…' she tucked her
hands under her legs, liking the way her thighs
squashed the tingling in her hands at the memory of Nick's ring on her finger '…too much
partying and drinking and getting into relationships and friendships that weren't healthy.'

Edwin shrugged. 'You were trying to work
things out.'

She exhaled, remembering how much it had
cut her to see Edwin's disappointment each time
he had learnt of yet another of her long litany of
disastrous acts and decisions in the years after
Michael's death. Studying him, she bit her lip,

wondering if she could dredge up the courage to ask the one question she'd always wanted to ask him, but never had the guts to—why he stuck around. She couldn't bear the thought that it was just because he pitied her. 'You were incredibly patient with me back then.'

Moving even further into his seat, he placed his forearms on his knees, his hands clasped, his gaze holding hers. Her heartbeat rose and rose as the seconds passed. 'You were hurting.'

She blinked. Nodded, her throat knotted with emotion. Was it losing his mother that made him so empathetic to how deeply she had grieved Michael?

'Once I graduated and moved here to Brighton for work, I thought for a while that I had my life under control. Mum and Dad's divorce had gone through and I wasn't having to constantly deal with their arguments. I was enjoying work and I had my own little flat, which I loved. But I knew nobody here in Brighton. And then you moved back to Monrosa.' Picking up her teacup, she held the warm porcelain in her hands. 'With you out of the country I didn't even have someone to give me earache about my lack of judgement.'

Edwin smiled. 'Not earache, guidance.'

With a deep inhale she admitted, 'And then I met Nick. He seemed to be everything I was looking for—really attentive, and he wanted to be with me all the time. Our relationship made me feel safe.'

She shuffled her chair a few inches away from the fire, a burning, embarrassed heat flaming inside her, knowing she needed to continue her explanation as to why relationships terrified her. 'It's hard to explain, but over time I began to realise that he was just too into me. He was constantly texting and calling me. Most evenings he came around here. He'd get angry when I had to work late or if I wanted to go out with work colleagues. He started to call me several times a day. Wanting to know where I was and who I was with. He said he called just to make sure I was okay. And then about a year into our relationship he entered a phase where he'd blow all hot and cold. One day he'd be kind and attentive and the next day he'd totally ignore me. I never knew where I stood with him and it utterly confused me.'

Edwin's nostrils flared.

She could understand his anger.

She rubbed the back of her neck. Would she ever stop feeling embarrassed for being so clueless? Would she ever stop feeling somehow responsible for Nick's behaviour?

'My self-confidence took a dive. I lost all direction and sense of myself. I felt so confused.

You probably won't remember this, but you came to visit after you had attended a financial summit in London. You knew something was wrong, so I pretended I was sick and just generally stressed out by work, and you insisted I take some annual leave. You brought me back to Monrosa to stay in your family's villa in the mountains.'

'I remember. You said it was a virus—you never said anything about Nick.'

'I didn't really understand myself what the matter was. I just had this overwhelming sense of panic. So I thought it was something physically wrong with me—some type of stress response to missing my parents and being so busy with work. What I failed to face up to was how destructive my relationship with Nick was.' Kara swallowed at how Edwin's mouth was pulled into a tight line, anger sparking from his eyes.

'Why didn't you tell me?'

Because I didn't want you to know that I had messed up once again. I wanted you to see me as a peer. Not Michael's little sister who kept tripping up in life and needing your help.

'It was during my week in Monrosa that the idea to set up a charity started to form in my mind. I thought about Michael and how he struggled in university. And how I had struggled when I moved to Brighton, away from everything that was familiar to me. I wondered if there could be more support and awareness-building for young adults on managing major transitions and their mental health. I also faced up to the fact my relationship with Nick wasn't healthy, so I broke up with him when I returned to England.'

His eyes narrowing, Edwin asked, 'How did he take that?'

Grimacing, Kara admitted, 'Let's just say it took him a while to accept it.'

Edwin let out an angry breath. 'Did he harass you?'

'I had to block his number.'

Edwin sat forward, rolling his shoulders, his expression perplexed. 'Why didn't you ask for my help?'

'Pride and embarrassment, along with a dash of disbelief.'

Edwin threw his head back and studied the ceiling before returning his gaze to her. 'I wish you had told me.' Then, with integrity burning brightly in his eyes, he said quietly, 'I understand why you'd be cautious about getting into a relationship again and I swear to you I would never hurt you…but I get it, Kara. I'm not going to try to persuade you into something you don't want to do.'

Oh, thank God.

But boy, did she feel guilty.

'Is there anyone else you can ask?'

'There's no one else I can trust.'

She leant back in her chair feeling weak with the simple sincerity of his softly spoken words. 'I know how much this means to you.'

'It's my problem to sort out, not yours.'

'Can you challenge the new law your dad passed?'

'I've spent the past month trying to do just that. He's refusing to budge.' He stood and moved towards the door. 'I need to go back to Monrosa tonight.' Turning, he added, 'Thanks for listening and I hope you can understand why I asked you—people respond to you so positively. Despite what people might like to think, being a royal requires a strong work ethic, empathy and above all the ability to be a strong role model—and you have those qualities in bucket loads.'

Was that how he saw her? Really? Not the chaotic young adult who tested his patience endless times, or the charity CEO with a propensity to over-commit?

'I assume it'll be a temporary arrangement… if you find someone to marry.'

He paused and considered her for a moment. 'I can see no reason why it couldn't be permanent.'

'But what if you meet someone else? Actually fall in love?'

'I have liked being single and not being tied down, but that doesn't mean I won't stay true to my marriage vows. This may be a working marriage but I will respect the marriage even more for that. I will respect that whoever marries me will do so in good faith and deserve my utmost loyalty.'

Thrown, she asked, 'But what of your father's wish for grandchildren? How is that going to happen?'

A hint of a smile lifted on his lips. 'Are you asking me for a sex-education lesson?'

'No!'

'I've told my father he may have forced my hand in marrying but that he has no say in whether or not I have children.'

'How did he react to that?'

'He was surprisingly unperturbed. I can't help but think he didn't want to give away his annoyance that he hadn't included the need for children to be born in the marriage to be part of the succession rules.'

Edwin left the room and, lost for words, Kara studied her hands. They were shaking. How hadn't she noticed that before now? His footsteps echoed on the tiles of the kitchen floor. He came back into the sitting room, shrugging on his jacket. She moved in the chair to stand. He gestured for her not to.

As usual he went to give her a hug goodbye.

But rather than hug her for the normal quick squeeze they usually shared, he laid his hands gently on her shoulders, their warmth seeping into her bones, his cheek brushing against her hair. Pinpricks of awareness bubbled on her skin. An air of sadness, almost vulnerability, surrounded him.

She went stock still. How much must it have taken Edwin to ask her to marry him—this proud, self-sufficient man who never asked for help or support? A whoosh of admiration for him hammered through her. Edwin would have agonised over this and would not be asking her to marry him lightly. He *really* mustn't have another option. She knew what it meant to him to succeed to the throne. All his ambitions for Monrosa. Her head swam with all the reasons why saying no was the only sane thing to do. But how could she turn him down when he had been her lifeline so many times before?

He straightened. Her heart beating like a trapped butterfly, she tried to keep her voice steady. 'I'll give you two years. After that we can divorce. Anything less would seem…unbecoming.'

'Are you saying yes?'

'I think so.'

Edwin pulled her into a hug, his arms holding her tight. Her head swam again. His chest was solid warmth, his scent the usual reminder of the mountain forests of Monrosa.

When he pulled away his gaze held hers. 'I need to leave for my flight. Think about your answer overnight. Call me tomorrow. I don't want you rushing into a decision you may later regret.'

With that he left the room and a few seconds later she heard the front door open and quietly shut. She let out a long exhale and clenched her shaking hands. Her gaze ran around her sitting room. This was her home. Was she really prepared to move away from this life she had built for herself to live in a country where she would know no one other than her pretend husband?

CHAPTER THREE

KARA ATTEMPTED TO join the other early Monday morning joggers as they ran along the promenade, but after a few hobbled steps she gave in to the tightness in her thigh.

It was still dark, a heavy mist dancing around the street lights. She should have stayed in bed. But her jumbled thoughts had needed air.

Last night she had created a pros and cons list for marrying Edwin when she hadn't been able to sleep. On the cons side she had listed in no particular order of importance:

Losing my privacy
Leaving my job and home
Moving to a new country
The media sensation when we marry and divorce
I have no idea what is involved in being a princess and I'll just mess up
My parents' disapproval—they might like

*Edwin, and in truth not show much inter-
est in my life, but I can't see that stopping
them having conniptions to see their only
child agreeing to such a public and high-
profile pretend marriage*
Having to fake being in love in public
The damage it could do to our friendship

On the pros side she had put:

It could be fun??

But she had crossed that out for being too
frivolous and then had written in capital letters
two single points:

It's my turn to help Edwin
*It will give me the platform to raise the
international profile of Young Adults Together*

On a daily basis, the Young Adults Together
internet forums received messages from people
from all over the world looking for help and support. And the only way to ensure they reached
as many people as possible was for local communities to get involved in the charity's work
and fundraising.

It hadn't taken her long to realise that the cons

side of the list was heavily weighted towards the impact of accepting Edwin's proposal would personally have on her. While the pros side was about her giving back. It was no contest really.

However, there was an extra con she hadn't even been able to write down last night, hating to think that Edwin was anything like Nick, but what *if* he was manipulating her? Just as Nick had used to do. Was he using her to antagonise his dad or perhaps to divert the media's attention away from his succession to the much juicer speculation as to just why he had chosen her to be his bride? She knew she could trust Edwin—for crying out loud, he had done nothing but support her for the past decade... but that nagging doubt was still there.

Cheers, Nick. You've really managed to make me paranoid about everyone's motives.

Hobbling back to her apartment, she knew she had to make a decision. Edwin deserved a final answer from her.

Opening the front door, she went towards the kitchen, where she had left her phone charging last night. By the hall table she paused at the collage of photos on the wall, realising it had been a long time since she had stopped to look at them.

Her gaze sought out one particular picture amongst the dozen others.

Herself and Edwin and Michael, sitting in the beer garden of a pub in Oxford, wearing layers of clothes against the coldness of the winter's night, Michael sitting in between herself and Edwin, his arms thrown around their shoulders, staring into the camera, his expression earnest. Michael had approached life with an intense but passionate seriousness, as though he owed the world a debt. Had university triggered his depression or was it something he had always struggled with?

She blinked as tears washed over her vision, obscuring the photo of her two best friends.

She had lost one.

She wasn't going to lose the other. And she certainly wasn't going to let Nick's behaviour influence her decision either.

Edwin answered immediately. 'Hi.'

His voice was low and husky. Was he still in bed?

Edwin lying in bed... Did he wear pyjamas? Somehow she couldn't imagine him pulling them on. Wait... What exactly would their living and sleeping arrangements be when they married?

Despite her throat being suddenly tighter than her dad's wallet, she said in a tumble of words, 'My answer is still yes. I'll marry you. I'm assuming I'll need to move to Monrosa... but then what?'

There was a pause on the other end of the line. 'I'm glad.'

Her heart galloped at the reserved relief in his voice. She could hear a rustling sound of paper and then the soft tread of footsteps. She had been wrong. He wasn't in bed. Was he having breakfast, in his office? Then he spoke again. 'After we marry we will use the royal apartments within the palace. The south-wing apartments have been recently renovated and will suit us perfectly. There's an office there with a balcony that overlooks the mountains that will be perfect for you.' He paused. She could hear his footsteps again. And then he sighed. 'We'll need to share a bedroom, and a bed —our staff are usually very loyal but sometimes there can be a rogue insider who informs the media about our personal lives.'

Was he serious? Share a bed!

'How big is the bed we'll be sharing?'

'It's an antique four-poster.'

Any antique beds Kara had ever come across were always on the miniscule size. 'How big?'

Edwin cleared his throat, but not before she heard him chuckle. 'I guess you could say it would be a cosy fit for two.'

She huffed. And was grateful he couldn't see her red cheeks right now. 'Order a new bed and make it a super-super-king-size.'

She ended the call to his laughter.
And then she laughed too.
Had she lost her mind?

Wednesday afternoon and the usually tranquil white drawing room of Monrosa Palace, with its walls draped in white and gold silk brocade, fragile French gilt-bronze furniture sitting on handwoven silk rugs, reverberated with impatient mutterings.

'This atmosphere is more akin to that of a funeral than an engagement announcement,' Edwin muttered to Victor, his personal secretary.

Victor eyed the rest of the room. Alongside Edwin's father, who was getting increasingly agitated at the delay in starting the afternoon's proceedings, the Secretary of State, the First Aide de Camp to His Royal Highness, the Chamberlain and various other advisors close to His Highness had assembled for the engagement announcement. And clearly none were happy with his father's earlier declaration in a private briefing that he was going to abdicate the following day.

'His Highness has ruled Monrosa for thirty-five years. We are a conservative society. In time the people will accept his decision,' Victor replied with his usual understated diplomacy.

Turning his back on the room, Edwin studied the news reporters gathered at the far end of the internal courtyard of the palace. The palace, once a Moorish fortress, had been extended and renovated by practically every generation of the Prado family, which had ruled Monrosa for the past six hundred years. His ancestor, Prince Louis II, had erected a low arched gallery supported by three hundred and sixty-five marble pillars around the internal parameter of the courtyard. His father's contribution had been to commission the restoration of the frescoes painted by Miotto and Formano in the south wing of the palace.

Even from the opposite side of the vast courtyard, originally constructed with another enemy in mind, Edwin could sense the media's anticipation that something of importance was about to happen. His father addressed the press every Thursday afternoon. Only something of major significance would warrant a separate press gathering the day before.

It's about to happen.

He balled his hands and breathed deeply into his diaphragm. He needed to ground himself, banish every reason why he didn't want to do this and focus on the succession. Too much thinking and ruminating got you nowhere.

The mumbling behind him had ceased.

He whipped around.

Standing with his aunt, Princess Maria, at the threshold of the room, her hair straightened into sleek waves, her professionally applied make-up emphasising the blue depths of her eyes, Kara stood scanning the room, until her eyes locked with his.

She gave him a nervous smile.

He winced at her unease.

Her forest-green below-the-knee fitted dress had a deep slash from her collarbone to the centre seam, and her hand rose to touch the exposed pale skin of her breastbone.

Her dress was perfect. She was perfect. With her irresistible wide smile and rose blushed cheeks she was what every royal bride was supposed to be.

The only problem was that she was a reluctant bride, only going through with a marriage of convenience in a selfless act of friendship.

Kara's description of her relationship with Nick Green had knocked him for six. He gritted his teeth, once again seething that he hadn't taken the time to unearth why he had never taken to Nick. Instead he had shrugged off that instinct that said there was something insidious about him and had put it down to him just being protective of Kara. He had tried to be chilled about their relationship, pleased for her, when in fact his skin had crawled at the thought of them being together.

But the truth of Nick's controlling personality wasn't the only reason he was so thrown— in Kara revealing the truth, for the first time it had dawned on him that Kara might want greater intimacy between them. What he had thought would be a simple marriage of convenience hadn't allowed for the needs and vulnerabilities that came with any relationship. What if Kara continued to confide in him and expected in return an emotional intimacy he wasn't capable of giving? Just because she had never looked for it as a friend didn't mean that would continue when they were husband and wife.

Michael would have freaked to see his little sister put in this position. Guilt and unease twisted inside him—he knew what he was asking of Kara, the huge sacrifices she was having to make in order to help him to the throne. *Dio*, he hated having to ask for her support—it was selfish, and it felt as though his world order was turned upside down. It was his role in their relationship to be the supporter, the one in control. He didn't want to be dependent on anyone, even Kara. He liked to be autonomous and detached from others. Emotional intimacy terrified him. It was the reason why all of his past relationships had ended. He had always backed away from letting anyone too close. He could never deal with the pain of losing someone he loved again.

Behind him his father called out, 'Maria, I told you not to delay us.'

While the rest of the room, including Kara, was startled at his father's barked reprimand, his aunt gave him one of her serene smiles and, ushering Kara into the room, said, 'The media can wait. Kara and I had some important matters to talk over, including selecting a dress created by a Monrosa designer for the engagement photos.

'What do you think, Edwin? Doesn't Kara look beautiful?' Not waiting, thankfully, for him to answer, his aunt spoke to her husband, Johan. 'Do you remember just how excited we were when we announced our engagement?' Looking back towards Kara and then him, she clapped her hands in excitement. 'Enjoy every moment of this very special time in your lives.'

His aunt, who knew nothing about the truth as to why they were marrying, waited for a response. Only his father, brothers and Kara's parents knew the true reason for their marriage. The fewer people who knew the truth, the better. Struggling to find an appropriate response, he obviously hesitated too long in giving a reaction because his aunt's expression shifted to one of confusion.

Before he had an opportunity to speak his father barked, 'We have much more important matters that need to be taken care of other than worrying about dresses.'

Kara stepped forwards with a conciliatory smile and addressed his father. 'I apologise for the delay, but I do agree with Princess Maria. My choice of dress will send out an important signal of my support for Monrosa.' She tilted her chin. 'It's inevitable, given the speed and nature of our engagement, that things will not always go according to plan one hundred per cent of the time, but I'm sure Your Highness will take that into consideration.'

His father reddened, not used to being challenged, even in such a polite way.

Edwin bit back a smile, proud of Kara's defiance.

Ever so subtly all of the others present in the room slipped to stand behind his father. Only he and Victor remained in the no-man's-land between Kara and his father.

Raúl, Director of Royal Communications, stepped forward and addressed His Highness with a pained expression. 'Sir, the press are waiting.'

His father eyed Raúl with exasperation and growled, 'Well, what are you waiting for? Go out there and start proceedings.'

Raúl nodded, squared his shoulders. About to leave the room, he doubled back and whispered, 'Miss Duffy, please try to remember your answers from our rehearsal this morning.' Turning to regard Edwin, who had moved over to stand next to her, Raúl added, 'I would suggest His Royal Highness is the one who answers any unrehearsed questions that might arise.'

Kara gave Raúl an uncertain smile. Her job required her to speak in public frequently, but Edwin knew it was her least favourite part of her role and one she was over-conscious and overly self-critical of. The last thing she needed now was somebody doubting her ability.

Edwin cleared his throat and stepped closer to Raúl. 'Miss Duffy is more than capable of answering any questions that might arise.' Edwin tried to eyeball Raúl but the other man's eyes shifted relentlessly in every direction but his. Biting back the temptation to sigh, Edwin added, 'I want some time with Kara alone before we speak to the media. Wait here for another ten minutes before you go out. We will be in the music room and will join you from there.'

Raúl, with a pained expression, peered back towards his father, who was now puce in the face.

'What's the delay now? Edwin, I command you to stop delaying proceedings.'

Edwin turned and approached his father. Those surrounding him remained where they were. A silence fell on the room. Edwin tilted his head and eyed each and every advisor one by one. They all understood he wanted to speak to his father in private. Was this their way of showing where their loyalty lay? Their concerns about his succession? Had he a rebellion on his hands? Seconds passed. He stood his ground. His father went to speak. Edwin shot him a look of warning. This was his battle. Eventually, no doubt realising that Edwin was prepared to wait for the rest of the day for them to retreat, the advisors slowly peeled away towards the back of the room. Edwin could only hope this was the start of the royal court accepting his authority.

Lowering his head, he addressed his father. 'Apart from a brief meeting earlier, I've spent no time alone with Kara since she arrived from London this morning. We need time to speak. I ask you to respect that.'

His father gestured out towards the courtyard. 'The media are waiting and we have important state matters to discuss. You can talk to Salma later.'

Edwin let out an impatient breath. 'You know damn well her name is Kara. And I don't care that you think I should have married someone with better connections and background. We are marrying because you have left me with no other option. But I will not cause any harm or distress to my bride.' As he held his father's gaze, years of frustration with his father's belligerence and uninterest in his family spilled out. 'Kara will soon be part of this family and, whether you like it or not, from now on we're going to act like one—this family has been dysfunctional for far too long. You are to respect Kara and her position. Never force me into a position where I have to choose between her and the crown.'

Whipping around, he guided Kara out of the room, a hand to her back, the need to protect her, to make sure she was okay, thudding through him like some primal beat.

Beneath his hand, her hips swayed as her high heels hit the marble floor of the anteroom. 'What did you say to your father? He looked even more hacked off than usual.'

She didn't know of his father's unhappiness at his choice of bride and he wanted to keep it that way. 'I apologise for his foul mood. He's anxious about tomorrow.'

Glancing behind her to the silent room, as all those gathered there watched their departure, she frowned. 'Is it always this tense around here?'

'At times.'

'I hope you'll instil a more positive atmosphere when you are in charge.'

'I aim to,' he hit her with a teasing smile, 'but then, you did say that my father and I are alike, so maybe I'll end up just as grumpy as him.'

'Not under my watch you won't.'

He laughed at her warning but there was something in her expression that had him realise that not only would she have his back in her role as his consort, but she would also push him to do the right thing, even if it was not what he always wanted to do. He wasn't quite sure whether to be comforted or alarmed by that.

Moving into the music room, he led her towards the terraced doors, where they were able to watch the media unobserved, thanks to the immense size of the Fountain of Bulls at the centre of the courtyard.

She sighed on spotting the assembled media, a hand unconsciously kneading the side of her neck. She was nervous.

'We'll be okay.'

She turned and studied him. 'Will we?'

His gaze shifted back to the media, remembering the morning after his mother's death. He had joined his father out in the courtyard for his address to the world's media. He had been bewildered and scared, barely able to comprehend that his mother was dead. He had pleaded with his father not to make him accompany him, but his response had been a brief lecture on his duty to the crown and country. To this day he could still feel the force of his need for his mother in that moment, for her words of encouragement and the hug she would give him whenever he had to perform a public duty.

Living your life so publicly was grindingly tough.

'I'll protect you from the media.'

Her hand dropped from her throat to hang by her side. 'It's not the media I'm worried about. It's us.'

Where had that come from?

'What do you mean?'

'For the past few days my calls to my local taxi company have lasted longer than our telephone conversations.'

'As I explained, I've been tied up with legal issues around the succession, and Aunt Maria has been tying me up in knots with her elaborate ideas for the wedding.'

Her pink-glossed mouth flatlined. 'Not *the* wedding, *our* wedding—we should be planning it together.'

'I didn't want to bother you with the details. I knew you'd be busy with your own work.'

That earned him a disbelieving look.

'This may only be a short-term marriage but I want an equal say.'

'Of course you'll have an equal say.'

'So why are you shutting me out?' she asked.

'I'm not shutting you out.' He wasn't, was he? Okay, so maybe he had been distracted in their phone calls over the past few days, but in his defence he was snowed under with things to organise…and there was also the small fact that he wasn't sure how to negotiate their new relationship as an engaged couple.

She raised an unconvinced eyebrow and turned to stare back out towards the media.

He ran a hand along his jaw and grimaced. 'The media will expect us to kiss.'

Her head whipped around.

Her eyes a startled blue, a blush crept up her throat and onto her cheeks.

He should reach out for her, draw her into a hug, tell her everything would be okay…but would it? No matter how much he would like to deny it, them kissing, the physical intimacy of it, was about to shift their relationship from straightforward friendship to a whole lot more complicated.

Kara kneaded her exposed collarbone. 'You don't have to kiss me if you don't want to.'

'I don't have a problem kissing you.'

She gave a tiny snort. 'Are you sure? You certainly don't sound too enthusiastic.'

'I don't want to put you in any situation you are uncomfortable with.' Despite himself he couldn't stop staring at Kara's mouth, the cupid's bow shape of her lips.

What would it be like to kiss her?

He arched his neck, a much too pleasant physical sensation trickling through his body.

Dios! *What was he thinking?*

She backed away from him, her expression flustered. 'I'm sure we can handle a quick chaste kiss.'

'Who said anything about it being chaste?'

She eyed him warily for a moment but then with a laugh, obviously deciding he was teasing her, she added, 'You're all talk—knowing how you like to keep your interactions with the media as brief as is humanly possible, I bet it will be a quick peck.'

'Is that a challenge?'

'No! Just an educated guess. Anyway, based on how badly I fumbled my answers when I had a practice run of questions with Raúl earlier, maybe us kissing will be a whole lot safer than having to answer questions. I have the real potential of putting my foot in it—you know how much I can prattle on when I'm nervous.'

'Be yourself. I don't want you to ever change

or feel the pressure to change. You're perfect as you are.'

She gave him an uncertain smile. *Dio!* That had come out all wrong. It sounded like an intimate, flirtatious compliment when it should have been just a statement of fact.

She turned her head to gaze around the room, taking in the antique musical instruments including a pianoforte and harp. 'I can't imagine myself roaming around here dressed in my pyjamas, eating a bowl of cereal any morning.'

'In our apartments you can do what you want.' He paused, and before he could stop himself he added, 'You can even roam around naked if it takes your fancy.'

Where the hell had that come from?

He raked a hand through his hair. Not only was he staring at her mouth in a whole new and inappropriate way, but now he was also inviting her to roam about their apartment naked. What was the matter with him?

She stared at him with her mouth open, but then rolled her eyes. 'I'd just put you off your breakfast.'

'Well, it'd certainly brighten up my day.'

Kara laughed but then, sobering, asked, 'What's going on? Are you trying to flirt with me in case I'm having second thoughts and might back out?'

Was she actually serious? 'Please tell me that you don't believe I could be so manipulative.' Pausing, he added, 'Are *you* having second thoughts?'

'No, but stop acting so weird. It's freaking me out. It's the kind of trick Nick would have tried on. I want to marry you. And how can I possibly not go ahead at this stage anyway, knowing I'd break your aunt's heart if I did? I had thought when she said she wanted to speak to me that it might turn out all Shakespearian and she'd try to persuade me not to marry you in a bid to gain the throne herself, but the complete opposite was true.'

Shaking his head at her vivid imagination, he pointed out, 'There are two important facts you need to know about my aunt—firstly, she hates public life and much prefers to spend her time attending to her gardens on her estate in the north of the island. And secondly, she is an incurable romantic. Planning a wedding is her idea of heaven. I haven't seen her so enthusiastic about anything in a very long time.'

'So I gathered. She also mentioned that your father's planning on moving to the north of the island also after he abdicates. Are you happy about that?'

That was a good question. 'I'll be able to stamp my authority more easily…'

She regarded him and then softly asked, 'But you'd like him to stay here?'

Was he naïve to think he would be able to drag his family back together? 'I know he might be a nightmare to have around but I want us to be a family, work together as a team.' There was a softness, a tender understanding in her eyes. She understood what it was like to have a family blown apart. 'It's what my mother would have wanted.'

Kara nodded and then, leaning against the terrace door, turning her back on what was going on outside, she studied him, her gaze drifting down over his navy suit. Nodding to his gold and purple tie, she said, 'The royal colours for the occasion.' Reaching out, she adjusted his tie a fraction. 'You're looking very handsome today. Your mother would be very proud of the man you have become.'

He swallowed at her words. *Dio*, he could only hope his mother would be proud of the man he was. When she had been alive he had always tried to make her proud and in death that hadn't changed. He wanted to emulate her care for Monrosa and its people. He wanted to keep her alive by his actions.

Out in the courtyard, Raúl hurried towards the media. No doubt under orders from his father to get the proceedings over and done with so that they could continue focusing on all of the issues arising from the impending abdication. 'The announcement is about to get underway.'

Twisting around, Kara watched Raúl. Her hand rubbed against her throat. Her fingernails were painted in a pale pink shade, the sapphire engagement ring he had presented to her earlier shimmering on her finger and disconcerting him with its unfamiliarity. With a wistful smile she said, 'I'm so glad you're going to try to get your family to be closer.'

With a sigh he pulled her in to him. As ever she held herself rigidly. 'I'm sorry your parents wouldn't be here today.' They had invited Kara's parents to be present at the announcement but both had declined, unhappy that Kara had agreed to a marriage of convenience.

She tilted her head so that her forehead rested lightly against his chest, the movement telling him everything he needed to know as to just how disappointed she was, and against her hair he whispered, 'I'll be your family now.'

She pulled back, her eyes glistening with tears. He touched his finger against her cheek, his heart pounding in his chest, emotion catching in his throat, at just how much he really meant those words.

But then with a shake of her head Kara pulled

back. 'Please don't say things like that, not when this isn't a real marriage.'

Taken aback by the vehemence in her voice, he asked, 'Why not?'

She twisted away, walked into the centre of the room, as though gathering herself. Whipping around, she answered, 'Because…because I've already lost one family…'

He inhaled deeply, the feeling of being way in over his head hitting him. 'You're not going to lose me.'

'Neither of us can pretend that our marriage is going to be easy. I don't think either of us can say that we'll come out of it unscathed. We need to be careful as to what we promise each other.'

A wave of frustration pushed through him. Kara was right. Wanting to kiss her, thinking they could be family…what was he thinking of? Raising his hands, he sighed. 'You're right.'

'What have you told Luis and Ivo?'

'Luis is in Australia at the moment and Ivo's in Budapest, competing, so I spoke to them both in a conference call this morning.' He paused and frowned. It had not been an easy call. 'Let's just say that once they got over the shock of learning that our father was going to abdicate, they were livid with him for forcing my hand and even more livid with me for dragging you into this mess.' Over the years Luis and Ivo had got to know Kara when they met in both London and Monrosa. Kara and Luis spoke regularly by text, their relationship one of endless teasing and banter, while Ivo was a goodwill ambassador for the charity, promoting its work within the sporting community.

'Wait, are you saying that they didn't know about your father's abdication until you told them?'

'He wanted to wait until tomorrow morning to inform them. I couldn't persuade him to tell them earlier. Things are as tense between him and my brothers as they have ever been.'

'Why won't he accept that they are both professional sports people who compete at an international level?'

'In his eyes they are wasting their time, when they should be here in Monrosa fulfilling their duties.'

She swept her hands over her dress, wriggling to smooth out the material clinging to her hips.

'Don't be nervous,' he reassured. 'You look incredible and I know you'll do great.'

'Aren't you nervous?'

From a young age he had been taught to present a public persona, one that was polite and composed and detached. That persona got him through so many aspects of his public life and was a shield behind which he could hide his true self. 'Why would I be nervous when I'm ready to celebrate my engagement with the world?'

She gave a disbelieving huff. 'Now you just sound corny.'

'Think of all the positives that can come from this—we can run together every morning and we can go hiking into the mountains without having to schedule it months in advance. We can watch movies together rather than just chat about them. And I can finally teach you how to sail.'

'You almost had me until you mentioned sailing. And what of the old adage, familiarity breeds discontent?'

'I think it's contempt, not discontent.'

Kara hit him with a teasing smile. 'I know, but I wouldn't go that far.'

'I want to marry you. And I hope that I'll be a good husband.' His chest tightened, a wave of emotion catching him unawares. 'I want to make you happy. If you are ever unhappy in the marriage then we can end it.'

'Even before the two years?'

Dio! What if she did walk away? Walked away because their marriage had gone horribly wrong? Their friendship destroyed. What if he had hurt Kara when he swore he would only ever protect her?

He clenched his hands. 'If that's what you

want.' Opening the terrace door, he asked, 'Are you ready?'

She gave him a nervous smile. 'With you at my side, what can go wrong?' And she stepped out onto the covered terrace.

A lot was the answer to that particularly hopeful question, as Kara soon found out.

As she stepped from the shade and obscurity of the courtyard gallery into the bright spring day and the glare of the world's media, her legs began to shake. All those eyes and cameras. Assessing. Already formulating words and images to describe her, to pass judgement on her.

And Edwin wasn't helping matters with his long stride. Through a clenched smile, she muttered, 'Will you please slow down? And shouldn't we be acting more coupley?'

Edwin came to a complete stop, his expression unreadable. Then, giving her that serious public smile of his that always swelled her heart with pride and affection for this honourable man who took his responsibilities so seriously, he tucked a strand of hair behind her ear and murmured, 'Is this "coupley" enough?'

At the periphery of her vision, reporters jostled each other for a better view of them, one reporter actually pushing another into a flower bed. She nodded frantically, worried Edwin might decide he should do something even more in his pretence of devotion.

He took her hand in his and they resumed their approach towards the reporters, her toes tingling from the sensation of his warm hand enclosing hers with an unnerving gentleness. Keen to distract herself from the endless walk across the vast courtyard, she whispered, 'My dad promised he'd try to watch the announcement on a livestream.'

Not breaking his gaze away from the media, Edwin whispered back, 'Once the abdication is over, we'll go and visit both of your parents. I'm sure we can persuade them to come to the wedding.'

'I've tried endless times during the past few days to talk them round.' Now was probably not the moment for this conversation but the need to offload her worry was too great—especially as she had been storing it up for several days, expecting to share it with Edwin on the phone, but his calls had always been cut short by some crisis or another. 'You know how private they both are—being in the public eye is their idea of a nightmare. And they think what we're doing is crazy—that it will never work. I've tried to tell them about all of the positives that can come from our marriage—raising the profile of the charity, your plans for Monrosa.

But they won't listen to me. We'll need to find a suitable explanation as to why they won't be at the wedding ceremony.'

With one easy movement, Edwin pulled them to a stop again.

Standing in front of her, blocking her from the media, he studied her while a silence descended on the courtyard, the assembled media holding their breath at the prospect of a sensational story unfolding.

'The media are waiting,' she whispered.

'Your parents have been through so much—I don't want to cause them any further distress. We really don't have to go through with this.'

For a brief moment, she was tempted to agree with him. God knew, she didn't want to create even more tension with her parents than already existed, but this marriage and all the publicity it would bring to the work of Young Adults Together was the most fitting way to make sense of Michael's death. She was doing the right thing. And in time, maybe her parents would come to understand that Michael, so passionate about helping others, would have wanted her to do everything possible to help those in need. Seeing the tension in Edwin's eyes, she tilted her head back. 'As I remember it, you've promised me a spectacular honeymoon—you can't back out of that now.'

Edwin studied her for a moment and then with a hint of a smile he turned around and led her towards the waiting media.

In his earlier briefing, Raúl had given her a thorough run-through of the engagement announcement procedure that had included showing her a photograph of each correspondent who would be permitted to ask questions. Sofia Belluci, the royal correspondent for the main state broadcaster, would be the first to speak to them.

'Congratulations, Your Highness.' Pausing, Sofia turned her attention to Kara with a hint of bafflement, and said, 'And to you, Miss Duffy.'

Beside her Edwin said in a clear, neutral voice with no hint of emotion, 'Thank you.'

'Your Highness, after so many years of knowing each other, why have you and Miss Duffy decided to marry now?'

'We've come to realise what we mean to one another.'

Sofia narrowed her gaze, clearly wanting a much more elaborate answer. 'Which is?'

Without missing a beat, Edwin answered, 'Kara is my best friend.'

God, he was good at this. To the point. Unemotional.

'And for you, Miss Duffy?'

She had practised her answer with Raúl endlessly this morning, but, opening her mouth to say all those practised lines, she paused and stared blankly at the media, whose sceptical stares were hardening by the second.

What were her lines...what had she agreed to say?

Tumbleweed moseyed through her brain. And then she blurted out, 'Edwin's my world.'

Oh, what? Why did you say that?

She'd sounded like a gushing teen fan who had just met her boyband idol.

Edwin, looked at her with a bewildered expression for a moment, but to his credit managed to somehow gather himself enough to place his hand tenderly on her cheek and gaze into her eyes, playing the in-love fiancé perfectly.

It was all pretence, of course, but to be gazed at with such unbridled affection had her struggling to breathe.

Edwin turned back to the media, his arm resting on her waist.

The microphone was passed from Sofia to a man in his late sixties, impeccably dressed. Óscar Collado, the major news correspondent from Monrosa's largest selling newspaper. And, according to Raúl, a man with a hound dog's scent for a story. 'How does His Royal Highness your father feel about your announcement...is he as surprised as the rest of us?'

Edwin stiffened beside her. 'Surprised? No.

In fact he's pleased that finally one of his sons is settling down.'

Óscar reflected on that answer for a while, clearly sizing up Edwin's tense demeanour and trying to decide if he should repeat the first part of his question, but instead he changed tack and asked, 'And how about your family, Miss Duffy?' Here Óscar paused as though searching for the right words. 'They must be truly amazed.'

It was clear what Óscar was insinuating. Edwin went to speak but she got there before him. With a gracious smile in Óscar's direction she decided to tackle this issue head-on. 'Edwin and I may come from very different backgrounds but our ideologies and outlook on life are very similar. We both value loyalty and friendship and serving others. It's our hope that people will be open-minded and supportive of us.'

Óscar gave an unconvinced smile to her answer. 'How do you think your late mother would have reacted to your engagement, Your Highness?'

Edwin's hold tightened, and he edged her in even closer to him. She swung her gaze towards him, tempted to whisper to him that he should refuse to answer a question that was so unfairly personal and intrusive.

Seconds passed as the media waited for Edwin to answer. Her heart flipped over to see Edwin's jaw working. She placed a hand on his, which was resting on her waist, and threaded her fingers between his. 'I believe my mother would have been delighted to have a daughter-in-law like Kara.'

He spoke with raw emotion in his voice. Taken aback by the sincerity of his answer, she had to force herself to concentrate on Óscar's next question. 'And the engagement ring—is it part of the royal collection?'

'No, it was especially commissioned,' Edwin answered.

She looked down at the sapphire ring Edwin had presented to her earlier that day. It was a stunning ring, an intense violet-blue stone mounted on platinum and surrounded by a cluster of diamonds.

At the media's beckoning she lifted her hand to display the sapphire.

And forced herself to smile.

Don't let the media see you're thrown. So what that he's given you a brand-new ring and not one from the royal collection? It was the sensible thing to do. For a marriage of convenience. Thinking he might not trust you with a ring from the historic royal collection or believe you aren't worthy of one...well, they're just silly thoughts. Aren't they?

When the media had finally had their fill of photographs, it was the turn of another journalist to speak, asking with a bright smile, 'Have you any message for the people of Monrosa, Your Highness?'

'I hope they will enjoy the wedding celebrations, which are currently being planned and will be announced in full in the coming week,' Edwin answered.

The female journalist swept her bright smile in Kara's direction. 'And you, Miss Duffy—do you have a message for the people?'

Oh, just that I'm terrified and not to judge me too harshly when we divorce. Oh, and, yeah— sorry to all of you who will be heartbroken to hear that one of the world's most eligible men is no longer available. Don't hate me for it—it wasn't my idea, honestly. At least you have the consolation that this has nothing to do with love or passion or any of those normal things.

'My message is that I very much look forward to living here in Monrosa and getting to know this beautiful country.'

The woman, in her early thirties, asked enthusiastically, 'And what will your role be when you marry?'

The journalist seemed genuinely interested

in her role, and, seeing an opportunity to talk about the charity, she answered, 'I will continue with my work for my charity, Young Adults Together, focusing on expanding its efforts internationally to promote the advocacy and support of positive mental health in young adults. But I also see my role as supporting Edwin at all times...' she paused there, at the point to which she had rehearsed with Raúl, but, seeing the journalist's encouraging nodding, as though willing Kara to say more, Kara found herself saying, 'especially during the transition...'

She stopped, her eyes widening, hot panic making her pulse thud wildly.

I almost gave away the abdication.

She stared blankly at the media as they all shifted forward in their seats with interest, that sixth sense of theirs intuiting a story. What was she supposed to do now? They were waiting for an answer. How on earth did Edwin think she was capable of taking on the role of princess?

Laying his hands on her shoulders, Edwin calmly finished her sentence, 'During our transition to married life. We have both led independent lives but we are looking forward to living together. I know Kara is excited to settle into palace life...' Pausing, his eyes alive with devilment, a smile tugging at the corners of his mouth, he added, 'She has a lot of intriguing plans for life in our private apartments.'

Kara reddened, a nervous giggle escaping.

The journalists gave each other a quizzical look as though wondering if anyone else got the joke.

With a pinched expression, Raúl swept in from where he had been watching proceedings at the side of the courtyard and spoke to the media. 'Thank you all for attending today's announcement. His Highness and Miss Duffy will now pose for more photographs.'

Edwin pulled her in closer to him. They embraced and smiled.

Maybe this was all they would want. No kissing required.

But no sooner had she had that thought than a chorus of, 'How about a kiss?' rang out from the assembled photographers.

Edwin turned her towards him.

Her stomach took a nosedive.

He leant down to her ear and whispered, 'Do you still think my kiss will be chaste?'

He drew back. She smiled at him nervously. And in return he gave her a wicked grin.

What had she started?

The teasing look on his face disappeared and suddenly he was looking at her with a heart-stopping intensity. This was no longer a game.

Time slowed down.

She fell into the golden depths of his eyes, only now realising there was a solid single fleck of brown in his right eye. What other secrets did he hold? A hunger to know him better swept through her.

Oh, help.

She needed to get a grip. He was her friend, her pretend fiancé.

Stop getting caught up in the crazy pretence of it all. This is not real.

His mouth lingered over hers.

His hands ran down the length of her arms, coming to rest at her elbows. The warmth of his touch had her sigh ever so lightly.

Something shifted in his eyes. A heat. A masculine heat.

His lips brushed against hers.

Firm and warm.

Light-headed, she swayed against him. Oh…oh…his heat, the hardness of his body, the electrifying rightness of all of him.

This is so wrong, but so right.

He pulled her closer, deepening the kiss, his arms wrapping around her, tilting her backwards.

This wasn't a polite kiss. It was personal. Intimate. His taste, his scent, the heat of his skin against hers was perfectly wrong.

Every cell in her body dissolved to nothing and fire burnt along her veins.

No man had ever had this effect on her.

Oh, please...this can't be happening.

Her pretend fiancé seriously couldn't be the hottest kisser ever. This wasn't fair!

She willed him to keep on kissing her and he obliged by twisting her so that she was hidden from the media, his back to them, and he deepened the kiss even more, exploring her mouth.

Her hands clasped the hard muscle of his neck. Any moment now she was going to burst into flames. They should stop. This was crazy. Beyond madness to be doing this in the glare of the media. But she just couldn't pull away. One more second. One more spine-tingling, head-spinning, belly-warming second. One more thrilling, life-affirming second of hot craving zipping along the length of her body.

Edwin ended the kiss. And studied her up close for a moment, his pupils dilated, heat on his cheeks.

Dazed, she stared at him. Why did he look so different? More handsome, more male...he had always been gorgeous but now there was a raw edge to him that spoke of danger...of lust. Of... Crikey, what was happening to her?

Turning to the media, Edwin gave them a

nod before he led her away, much too quickly, across the courtyard.

When they were out of earshot he said, 'You're trembling.' His mouth tightened. 'Forgive me, I got a little carried away proving that I don't do chaste kisses.'

She had to downplay this. She couldn't let him know just how disconcerted she was, how he had just blown her mind.

So tell me, Kara, are you still convinced that you can walk away from this pretend marriage unscathed?

She withdrew her hand from his, gave him a disapproving tap on his forearm, and in the best blasé voice she could muster, answered, 'I could hardly breathe. Thank goodness we won't need to do that too often.'

CHAPTER FOUR

STANDING IN THE hall lined with mirrors, over-looking the formal gardens of the palace, spotting the telltale claret-red patches appearing on her dad's neck, Kara edged closer to him. 'I wonder what Aunt Joan will be wearing today?'

For a brief moment her dad smiled. 'Whatever it is, I'm sure they'll be able to spot it from outer space.'

Aunt Joan liked to wear colour, the brighter the better in her view, to counteract the greyness of so many Irish days. Unfortunately she didn't seem to understand the concept of clashing colours or that sometimes, less was more. Keen to keep her dad distracted in their long wait for Edwin to appear, and in truth looking for something to focus on other than her annoyance with her fiancé, she said, 'It's great that the entire family could make the wedding.'

When had the deep grooves in his cheeks appeared, the greyness in his hair? She hadn't seen him in over two years. Had it been during that time or had they been accumulating for ever and she had just been too preoccupied to notice? Her dad tugged at his shirt collar. 'Sure, wild horses wouldn't have kept that lot at home—this is the most exciting thing to have ever hit the Duffy family.'

Yesterday lunchtime they had finally managed to squeeze in the wedding rehearsal. Not only had the logistics team had to contend with Edwin's father's schedule, which had him out of the country on a tour to Sweden and Norway from which he had only returned yesterday morning, but also Edwin's ever-changing travel plans.

She had found the rehearsal in the cathedral exhausting. It had taken all of her will not to stare at Edwin, as was her wont recently. Since their engagement kiss she was constantly finding herself staring at him, daydreaming about him in all types of inappropriate ways that certainly didn't belong in a place of worship.

At the rehearsal her dad had trembled as he had escorted her down the aisle. In the hope of relaxing him she had said she and Edwin would join him and the rest of her relatives for dinner that night in the nearby hotel the palace had booked out in entirety to house the Irish Duffy contingent for dinner. She had also invited along her bridesmaids—Siza, her old rugby team-mate, and Triona, who was the first employee to join her in Young Adults Together, and was now one of her closest friends—who were also staying in nearby hotels.

She had ended up going for dinner without Edwin. His weekly meeting with the cabinet had apparently become heated when he introduced his plans for designating land zoned for tourist accommodation into a financial centre and nature reserve.

During the dinner she had tried to hide her frustration with Edwin's non-appearance, but when her dad had asked her for a chat after dinner she had expected yet another awkward conversation as to the wisdom of her deciding to agree to a marriage of convenience.

But instead, when they reached his room her dad had shyly plucked out the lightweight suits and crisp shirts he had bought for the wedding weekend. Her heart had melted to see how proud he was of his purchases, and how eagerly he had wanted her approval. He had asked for her advice as to what he should wear for today's garden party and had proudly modelled the grey trousers and pale pink shirt she had picked out. He had self-consciously studied himself in the full-length mirror of the wardrobe and it had hit her once again what it was she was asking of this private man, whose confidence and identity had taken such a battering, to have to step into the glare of the world.

Now with a grimace her dad admitted, 'I think you should know that your aunts gave an interview to one of the main Irish newspapers. I saw it online earlier in the special supplement they've published in advance of the wedding tomorrow.'

Kara groaned.

'It's all very complimentary...honestly, just photos of you growing up and how proud they are of you and how they knew you'd do great in life because you were such a headstrong child.'

Oh, please, someone tell me they didn't use the photos of me on the beach close to Aunt Nina's house with a battalion of cousins.

The photos where her hair was twisted into tight curls and stood on end like hundreds of startled question marks, thanks to a day spent in the sea.

So much for asking that family members wouldn't speak to the media. She didn't want her family or friends to be invested in this marriage. Unfortunately she had forgotten just how much her dad's side of the family liked a wedding, not to mention a royal one featuring their very own niece.

She couldn't even bear to think about just

how crushed they'd all be when her divorce was announced. 'Am I right in guessing it was my aunts who eventually persuaded you to come to the wedding?' It was only last week that her dad had finally said he would attend, a fortnight after the rest of their Irish family's acceptances had started rolling in.

Her dad gave a resigned sigh. 'Five badgering sisters would be hard for any man to fight.'

She twisted Edwin's engagement ring, its weight still feeling alien on her finger, regret punching her stomach that her dad was only here because of family persuasion and not to support her in her decision, even if it was not one he approved of. But at least he was here... which was more than could be said for her mum.

'I blame myself,' he said.

'Blame yourself for what?'

He looked her in the eye, the intimacy of it swiping like a blade to her heart. How she missed his easy nature and love of teasing that had used to have her giggling endlessly as a child. 'If we were closer...' He paused, shrugged. 'We've drifted apart, haven't we?' He nodded unhappily towards their opulent surroundings, and then in the direction of Edwin's father and brothers and the various other members of the royal court standing to their side. 'If I knew what was going on in your life then maybe I could have persuaded you not to do this before it all got so out of hand.'

Kara rolled her shoulders and placed her bunched hands in the pockets of her summer cocktail dress.

This morning she had hopped out of bed, thrilled that she had finally persuaded Edwin last night, when he had eventually turned up at her dad's hotel, two hours late, to take an early morning trek with her into the mountains. She had hoped some time alone together would restore the equilibrium that had used to exist between them, that some teasing and banter would fix Edwin back into her world order of regarding him as a friend. But her hope and excitement had soon disappeared when she had gone in search for him. Unable to locate him, she had been forced to interrupt Victor, who had been in a meeting with many of the senior members of the household, to enquire as to Edwin's whereabouts. Curious eyes had studied her, everyone present clearly wondering why she did not know that her fiancé had left Monrosa earlier that morning. She had tried not to let her embarrassment, her disappointment, her confusion show but had backed out of the room, her cheeks stinging with hurt.

And after her make-up and hair had been completed by her team and she had pulled on

the strapless dress she had fallen in love with
the moment Ettie, a recent design-school graduate and native Monrosian had shown it to her,
and stared at her reflection in the mirror, taking in the material printed in layers of pinks
and purples and yellows, designed to resemble
the colours and pattern of a butterfly's wings,
she had stared at the stranger in the mirror and
wondered if she could go through with the wedding. But what choice did she have? How could
she back out now with most of their guests already here? And on what basis—that Edwin
was never around, and even when he was he
was constantly distracted by work? With a sigh
she faintly said, 'Let's not go over all this again,
Dad. You know the reasons why I want to marry
Edwin.'

'A marriage without love destroys people.'

She did not want to hear this right now. She
had enough on her plate without her dad proph-
esying doom and gloom for their marriage. She
had enough of those niggling doubts herself.
'We might not have romantic love, but there's
no one in the world I trust more than Edwin.
He has always had my back.' Shifting her head
even closer to her dad, she whispered with a
fury that rose suddenly and fiercely from somewhere deep inside of her, 'He has never let me
down. I owe him this.'

Her dad blinked. And just as quickly as it had risen within her, Kara's fury was quenched, to be replaced with those nagging doubts that had been germinating like a deadly virus inside of her following weeks of Edwin's distraction and distance.

Her dad reddened. 'I wish your mother were here to speak to you. She might be able to get you to see sense.'

Kara shrugged. It hurt like hell that her mum was refusing to take the short plane trip from the south of Spain to Monrosa to attend her wedding, but she was *not* going to admit that to anyone. 'Maybe it's for the best—the last time you two were in the same room it wasn't exactly a pleasant experience for anyone.'

Her dad cleared his throat, stuffed his hands into his trouser pockets, his gaze on the closed double doors out to the gardens. 'You can't spend your days and nights with someone and remain detached. Edwin is a good-looking man… I don't want you getting hurt.'

Her mouth dropped open. Was her dad actually warning her not to sleep with Edwin? Heat ignited in her belly as she remembered their kiss. A few weeks ago she would have been able to laugh off her father's warning, but now she became a physical wreck of hormones whenever she saw him. She fancied him. She really,

really fancied him. He was that good a kisser. 'I wouldn't worry if I were you—if the past few weeks are anything to go by, we'll rarely see one another.'

'Victor, where is Edwin? Our guests are waiting for us.'

Both she and her dad jumped at Edwin's father's barked question that echoed around the cavernous double-height hall ceiling like a helter-skelter in motion.

Victor stepped away from the marble pillar beside which he had been standing and calmly answered, 'His plane landed ten minutes ago, Your Highness. He should be arriving very soon.'

Eyeing Kara as though it was her fault Edwin was late for his own pre-wedding garden party, Edwin's father asked, 'Just how urgent was the business that took him out of Monrosa? Doesn't he realise he's getting married tomorrow and is needed here?'

For a moment Kara was tempted to fire back, *Don't look to me for answers. I've no clue as to what's going on in your son's head. All we've talked about in recent weeks is wedding logistics and succession planning. Heaven knows he's never been good at talking about anything of even a slightly personal nature, but since our engagement he's taken it to a whole different level.*

But instead she gave him a polite smile and answered, 'I'm sure it must be of great importance, as he would not have wanted to keep our guests waiting.'

His Highness muttered something before turning his attention on Luis, who was leaning against the wall, his shoulder touching the gilt frame of a no doubt priceless still-life, flicking through his phone, and snapped, 'Please focus on our important guests this afternoon.'

A grin formed on Luis's mouth. He got the poorly disguised insinuation of his father's words—not to get sidetracked by pretty female faces, as was his wont. 'Don't take your bad mood out on me.' His grin dropping, Luis eyed his father, the roguish prince with a reputation for short-lived affairs with some of the most beautiful women in the world now replaced with the astute professional sportsman who had come close to winning the World Powerboat Series on several occasions. 'This whole mess is of your own making—no wonder Edwin doesn't want to play ball.'

Every eye in the room swung in Luis's direction, everyone clearly trying to understand the meaning of his words.

Tight-lipped, His Highness stared at his middle son furiously. 'Your constant absence from palace life has caused you to forget the importance of decorum.'

Luis held his father's gaze for long seconds, the heat in his cheekbones in stark contrast to the coldness of his expression. He shot his gaze in her direction. Kara gave him a supportive smile, all the while hoping he wouldn't start an argument that would add even more tension to the day. With a reluctant shrug Luis lowered his head and once again flicked a finger over the screen of his phone.

His Highness let out an irritated breath before turning his attention towards Ivo. 'I've scheduled time in my diary on Monday morning for us to meet.'

Ivo, with his tall, muscular physique, short-cropped hair and sharp features, on the surface appeared confidently aloof, but his low voice told the truth of his gentle nature. 'I'm flying out on Sunday morning.'

'Well, change your plans,' His Highness countered.

With zero emotion showing, Ivo studied his father for a moment. Kara expected him to refuse to change his plans. Ivo might be gentle but he had a stubborn and single-minded streak, which had served him well, no doubt, in his journey to becoming an Olympic rower. After a quick glance in her direction, rather surprisingly, he shrugged in agreement.

Walking towards a window overlooking the gardens, Kara studied their waiting guests down at the waterfront, her eyes brimming with tears. Edwin's distance stung even harder in the face of his brothers' understated support.

There were over five hundred guests mingling at the waterfront awaiting their arrival. Along with heads of state and prime ministers, local people and Young Adults Together staff were among the invited guests. She had had to fight hard the resistance of the wedding logistics team to have them invited ahead of corporate presidents and European politicians.

She had had to fight too for her idea to hold this garden party in the afternoon before the wedding. The logistics team had argued that many of the guests, especially those designated as dignitaries, would not arrive until the morning of the wedding and therefore the garden party was unnecessary and would only complicate preparations for the following day. Time and time again, Kara had had to remind them as to why she wanted to host the garden party in the first place—it was Kara's way of including as many Monrosians in the wedding celebrations as possible and her way of thanking those who had taken the time and expense to travel from all over the globe for the long weekend of celebrations.

As it had turned out, many of the dignitaries had opted to travel to the wedding early, and who could blame them for starting their weekend early on a sun-kissed Mediterranean island ablaze with colour, thanks to the springtime blooming of its native wild plants and flowers?

A number of guests had been unable to accept their invitation due to work commitments or personal issues. Only one had not sent an apology, however: her mum.

Kara had spoken to her only once since their engagement photos had been splashed across the front page of every newspaper worldwide. The pain in her mum's voice when she had begged Kara not to ask her again to attend the wedding had torn through her like a sharp blade. Kara knew just how private her mum was but had hoped she would have put that aside for her sake. In the reporting of their engagement, the media had referenced Michael's death, more often than not as a small aside paragraph at the end of an article, as though his death had been nothing but a blip in their lives.

She had gasped when she had seen the photos herself, grown all hot and bothered at the ones showing Edwin passionately kissing her. But it had been one photo—a fluke, a misinterpretation due to the angle at which it had been taken, but unfortunately the photo used by most of the media outlets—that still cut her to the quick. The photo had been taken in the seconds after Edwin had drawn back from their kiss, and the media had chosen to deduce from the intensity of his expression that it portrayed a man deeply in love.

When in truth it was nothing more than the portrayal of a man deeply irritated with himself. He regretted that kiss. He hadn't even been able to look her in the eye since. Which was mortifying, considering the lust it had unleashed in her. And any fears she had had about them sharing an apartment were a joke. Edwin had been away on business most nights since she had moved to Monrosa a fortnight ago. She had tried to shrug off his constant work and royal commitments abroad, burying herself in wedding preparations and in managing the transition of the day-to-day operations management of Young Adults Together in the UK to Marion Parry, her Head of Charity Services, so that she could focus instead on forming an international branch of the charity.

But despite her busyness, and how excited she was at the prospect of helping even more young adults, deep down she was lonely.

Was this how the next two years were going

to pan out? Edwin consumed by work, their relationship nothing more than work colleagues who saw each other occasionally? Her spending her nights alone, rattling around their enormous apartment trying not to have sexual fantasies about her indifferent husband? Their friendship lost to the careful dance they needed to perform every time they stepped out to fulfil a public duty, lost to the exhausting toll of keeping up the pretence of being a couple in love, lost to Edwin's ceaseless drive to prove wrong all of the commentators who proclaimed that his succession was happening a decade too early?

His father's abdication announcement had been received with shock and disquiet, the media and public unsettled by what the change in leadership would mean to the country. Ever since, Edwin had been waging a campaign, both at home and abroad, to bring people on board with his succession.

'Edwin, about time.'

Her neck snapped back at His Highness's snarled chastisement. Whipping her head around, she felt her heart leap to see Edwin filling the entranceway, dressed in navy trousers and a white shirt, the top button undone to reveal the smooth, tanned skin of his chest.

His gaze swept towards her. She wanted to look away, to convey her annoyance at his lateness. But instead a rush of relief flooded her body, making her feel weak and light-headed. And then a charge of connection ran between them. A hunger for his company boiled in her stomach and blasted onto her skin.

It's as though he's a different person to the man I saw as my best friend.

She was noticing things about him she'd avoided seeing before—the powerful physicality of his body, the sharp height of his cheekbones, the firmness of his mouth.

He gave her a brief nod of acknowledgement and stepped to the side of the doorway, gesturing towards someone out in the corridor to join him.

And then he was protectively placing his arm around the woman who stood beside him.

Kara swallowed, disbelief punching away all thoughts. In a daze she moved across the room. Her light-headedness worsened. She swayed, her legs threatening to buckle beneath her. The outer edges of her vision darkened. Within seconds Edwin was at her side. Placing his arm around her, he pulled her against the strength of his body.

Together they faced her mother. Kara swallowed air greedily, drawing on Edwin's steadiness.

Her mum remained in the doorway, staring at

her with an intensity that stripped her soul bare. Her mum gave a tentative smile that spoke of a bucketload of anxiety and uncertainty. And the years of fighting and disappointments and isolation suddenly didn't compare to the tight emotion in her chest at the joy in seeing her mum.

She held her arms out nervously, wondering how her mum would react.

Her mum drew back on her heels.

Kara winced.

Her mum took a hesitant step forward.

And then another.

They hugged, her mum's embrace so familiar and yet uncomfortable due to its long absence. Kara drew back, the intensity of it all too much to bear.

She turned to Edwin. He had done this for her, had known, without her saying anything, that she wanted her mum at her side when she married. She held his gaze, this man who knew her so well, and blinked back tears.

'Kara?'

She turned back at her mum's soft whisper.

Her mum moved towards her and for a moment Kara was transported to her childhood bedroom and her mum's whispered wake-up call that was always accompanied with a soft stroke of her hair. 'Edwin is right, you know: you *are* going to need me, not just this weekend, but also when this is all over. Divorce is awful. No matter what the circumstances.'

Kara's heart sank. She tried not to wince. On the eve of their wedding Edwin wasn't thinking of their marriage. Instead, he was planning for their separation and divorce.

As one soon-to-be extended family they walked down through the terraced gardens towards their waiting guests. Edwin could feel a headache coming on. They were a family in name at least, but, given the tensions that existed within both his and Kara's families, using the term 'family' was probably an infringement of the Trade Descriptions Act.

This morning he had had to spend way too long persuading Kara's mother to join him on the return flight to Monrosa, telling her that Kara deserved her support even if she didn't agree with her decision to marry him.

That damned engagement kiss.

It had thrown a curve ball into his life, as powerful as a cricket ball whacking him on the head, and had sent him into a month-long dazed existence.

What had been supposed to be a staged kiss had transformed into a primal urge for more… more heat, more connection, more bodily contact.

But the after-effects—seeing how upset Kara

had been, the speculative calculation in his father's eyes when they had gone back into the palace, hating his constant urge, even weeks later, to pick up that kiss where they had left off, the conjecture in some of the media that a royal baby was bound to soon make an appearance after such an inflamed public display of passion, the texted messages demanding to know what the hell he was playing at from his brothers... all had led to him withdrawing into himself.

His behaviour was unsettling Kara. He had heard the disappointment in her voice every time he had called to cancel a planned trip to visit her in Brighton, and in more recent days, since her move to Monrosa, her attempts to appear unconcerned when he announced yet another long day of local meetings or another trip abroad.

But the constant questioning of his succession and its impact on Monrosa, the knowledge he had not only dragged Kara into this marriage of convenience but was also in danger of wrecking their friendship irreparably by having senseless fantasies of kissing her—and okay, he'd admit it, those fantasies contained a lot more detail than just kissing her—was spooking him. Fantasies that would wipe out a decade's history of a friendship built on trust and respect. As much as he wanted a more physical relationship with Kara, he knew taking that step would unravel a whole lot of emotions he was incapable of dealing with. He didn't want to compromise their friendship and most important of all he didn't want to hurt Kara. And right now he was trying to walk the exhausting and head-wrecking tightrope balance of not spending too much time with Kara while trying to continue to support her.

Last night, he had arrived late to her dad's hotel and she had bristled with irritation. But when her cousin Alice had sung a duet with her mother, Hilary, that irritation had melted away. The song had been upbeat and funny, the rest of the family howling with laughter, but despite Kara's forced smiles he had seen her loneliness in witnessing Alice and Hilary's close bond.

Now, as he led the party down towards the waterfront, given Kara's monosyllabic answers to his questions enquiring how everything was with her, he wasn't certain that persuading her mother to attend the wedding was the best idea after all.

Her hair was tied in a loose chignon, exposing her bare shoulders. A fragile chain hung around her neck. She was refusing to wear any jewellery from the royal collection and to date hadn't given him a satisfactory reason why.

As had become a recent habit of hers, her

thumb was twisting her engagement ring around her finger. *Why does she do that?* Was it to remind herself of its presence? Did it annoy her? He had spent hours with a jeweller commissioning it, wanting to create a ring that was uniquely hers, that spoke of his admiration for her.

Her make-up was soft and subtle, a sweep of mascara on her long lashes, shimmering pink on her lips, but there was a tension emanating from her that said she'd happily tear him limb from limb.

They were only minutes away from their guests. He needed to sort out whatever was irritating her. Now. Before their guests picked up on it.

Keeping his voice low, he leant in to her. 'I thought you'd like having your mother here.'

'Are you trying to offload me onto her?'

Where had that come from?

'I have no idea what you're talking about.'

She tilted her chin. 'My mother told me you believe I'll need her in the coming years—are you frightened I'll go to pieces when our marriage is over? Is that why you went and fetched her this morning?'

'Of course not.'

She gave him a disbelieving look. 'Then why did you?'

'Because a mother should be at her daughter's wedding. And I told your mother that you deserved her attention, not just for the wedding but all of the time.'

She shook her head and as they approached their guests she placed her hand on his elbow, the smile on her mouth not reaching her eyes, 'I'm going to pretend to believe you but I'll tell you this much: I'm certainly not prepared to spend this marriage with you avoiding not only me but also your family. I've no idea what's been bugging you recently but you need to get a grip before you turn into a grumpy emotional hermit.' She paused and grimaced, and on a low sigh she leant even closer to him. 'We both know the consequences of people shutting down.' Bruised, pained eyes met his. 'We have to learn from Michael...'

She walked away from him towards her charity team. His skin tingled with shame and guilt. She was right, of course. Isolating yourself rarely did any good for normal people in normal circumstances, but in the craziness of this pretend marriage keeping a healthy emotional distance was going to protect them in the long run. Yes, there would be short-term pain, but the long-term gains would far outweigh them.

Kara's team embraced her with excited exclamations, bringing her into their fold, until she disappeared from view.

Kara had insisted the garden party was to be an informal affair, much to the disquiet of his father's advisors. But she had stood her ground against their arguments, firm that the party should be a relaxed afternoon where the guests got to wear casual clothes and to mingle informally in a bid to be as inclusive and accessible as possible for *all* those attending, without the pressures dictated by royal protocol.

So without the necessity of formal introductions, his family filed away from him, his father approaching the President of the European Union, almost unrecognisable now in his short-sleeved shirt over linen trousers rather than his usual conservative suits. Luis went and greeted the US ambassador fondly, their old rivalry forgotten now that the ambassador had retired from powerboat racing. Ivo joined Princess Maria and Johan, who were in conversation with a young group of Monrosians all wearing the Monrosa Environmental Protection Agency T-shirts, the charity his mother had founded before her death.

Not only was he getting things wrong with Kara but all of his intentions to force his family to be a tighter unit weren't happening, thanks to the others' uninterest and frankly his own lack of effort. On a number of occasions he had suggested they all meet, but he hadn't pushed the issue when he only got excuses as to why they weren't available in response, or, in Ivo's case, no response at all.

He could blame his workload. His office was tantalisingly close to attracting a major German bank to locate in Monrosa and he was having to lead the final negotiations. And on top of that, there was the management of the wedding and succession planning, diplomatic phone calls that had to be made to international leaders, and daily briefings with the cabinet alongside his father where he was trying to stamp his authority, much to the reluctance of his father's loyalists. And his father's belligerence wasn't helping either.

He had told Edwin he wanted him to take over the day-to-day decision-making in the run-up to the succession, but then proceeded to question every directive he made.

So, yes, his workload was insane. But in truth he had been avoiding any personal interactions, even turning down Luis's and friends' attempts to persuade him to hold a bachelor party, needing time to get his head straight.

Kara's parents stood beside him, both glancing in the direction of her dad's side of the family, who weren't doing a particularly good job at hiding their surprise at Kara's mother, Susan's arrival. Kara's mother coloured and she turned as if to join Kara and her team but pulled back when the group erupted in laughter. Kara's father stepped towards her, gesturing towards his family. Kara's mother gave a pained smile but, straightening her shoulders, followed him as he led her towards his extended family. Could this weekend be the start of a reconciliation between Kara's parents? He sure hoped so. He was fed up with watching Kara's family letting her down. If they reconciled their differences then maybe they would give her the support and love she deserved.

He had *thought* Kara would be grateful to him for persuading her mother to come to Monrosa. But instead she had twisted his efforts to make it seem as though he had done so for reasons of pure self-interest. And as for Kara's contention that he was heading towards being a grumpy hermit—how was that even possible when he spent almost every waking hour in the company of others?

He stifled a groan.

His old work colleague from London, Laurent Bonneval, carrying his baby son, Arthur in his arms, his beaming wife, Hannah, at his side, was making a beeline in his direction.

After quick hugs, Laurent thrust Arthur into his arms, ignoring Hannah's protests to be careful. Arthur gave him a toothy grin.

Laurent chuckled. 'After all the babies you must have held in the line of duty, I'd have thought you'd have mastered the art of holding one at this stage.'

Laurent pushed against his arm, forcing him to relax and to allow Arthur's tiny frame to curl against his chest. Arthur chortled and reached for his shirtfront, clinging to him. Edwin stared down at Arthur's tiny hand gripping his shirt, a loneliness, a longing unravelling in his soul.

'Kara, it's so good to see you again.'

His head jerked up at Laurent's greeting.

Kara hugged Laurent—they had met on several occasions in London before Laurent had returned to France to take over his family business in Cognac—and then shook Hannah's hand when Laurent introduced his wife to her. Edwin had attended Laurent and Hannah's wedding last year.

'I always knew you two should be together,' Laurent said, looking at them both with an expansive grin. He threw his arm around Hannah and kissed the top of her head. With a grin that was frankly a little sickening in its serenity he added, 'I'm glad you've finally found your way to one another. Just like Hannah and myself after I almost messed everything up between us by breaking up with her and leaving London for France. It goes to prove that love will eventually win out, no matter how much we fight it!'

* * *

Three hours later, and an hour later than scheduled, Edwin marched back up to the palace, his
family and Kara trailing behind him.

At the Statue of Hera, he muttered a curse.
His father and Princess Maria were still on the
lower terrace, studying the wide swathe of ag-
apanthus that grew there and from a distance
resembled a stream of ice-blue water.

Had his family lost all sense of urgency?

Luis, idly climbing the wide steps of the terrace below, said something that had Ivo grin and
Kara cover her mouth to hide a smile, before all
three contemplated him and laughed once again.

When they eventually joined him, Luis gave
him a wink before he and Ivo continued their
climb back up to the palace.

Kara remained at his side and with a curious
look she asked, 'What's the matter? Didn't you
enjoy the party?'

'Three times I had to tell Luis it was time to
leave.' Edwin blew out an impatient breath. He
had had to insist that his family and Kara leave
the garden party so that the guests could be encouraged to make their way back to their hotels
and homes. Ricardo, the Master of the Household, had personally pleaded with him to bring
the party to a close, explaining he desperately

needed his serving staff to prepare for tomorrow's wedding banquet.

Kara backed away from him, giving a shrug. 'We were all enjoying ourselves.'

Her eyes were sparkling, her skin glowing, her pleasure at the success of the party twisting inside him so much that he was desperately tempted to push her against the granite plinth of Hera and kiss her happiness, touch his fingertips against the tender skin where her dress skimmed across her breasts.

Her breasts that swelled so perfectly.

Dammit, for years he had successfully ignored them. Even the times when they had gone sailing together and his eyes would burn with the effort of not staring at her when she'd stripped off to reveal a testosterone-surging bikini.

That kiss, and the fact that she was about to become his wife, were messing with his ability to see her as a friend only.

In silence they walked up the steps and into the hall of mirrors, where his brothers were waiting for them.

Luis was fixing his hair in the reflection of one of the mirrors. 'Ivo and I are taking you out for a drink tonight.'

Watching his father and aunt amble up the last set of steps to the palace, willing them to get a move on so that he could say his goodbyes to them, Edwin answered, 'I have other plans.'

Angling his head to better inspect his newly grown beard, Luis responded, 'Well, change them. You can't get married without some form of a bachelor party. Even if it's not a real wedding.'

Their father, now standing at the doorway from the terrace, growled, 'At least Edwin understands the meaning of duty.'

Luis cocked an eyebrow. 'You more or less put a gun to his head. Edwin doesn't want to marry. We all know that. You've given him a life sentence.' Turning, he gave Kara one of his trademark cheeky smiles. 'No offence, Kara, but you know what I mean.'

Kara gave him a half-hearted smile.

Right. He'd had enough. Luis's constant rebuking and bickering with his father was one thing, but this was just plain offensive to Kara.

'Cut it out, Luis.'

Luis twisted around, his arms shifting outwards in question. 'Are you seriously taking his side now?'

Edwin looked from Luis to his father, both angling for an argument, and then to Ivo, who had turned his back on them all to stare out of the window in the direction of the harbour. Aunt Maria appeared from the terrace, cradling a bunch of purple irises in her arms, frowning as she picked up the tension in the air. It was time they all went their separate ways before things kicked off.

He shifted towards the doorway. 'I have work to do.' Then, looking in Kara's direction, taking in once again the sexy slope of her exposed shoulders, imagining his lips on her skin, imagining releasing her hair and coiling it around his fingers, imagining her wearing nothing but the pink sandals on her feet, he backed even further away, his body temperature surging. 'I'll see you tomorrow…at the cathedral. Enjoy your meal with your parents tonight.'

Kara's gaze narrowed. And then she was stalking towards him. Chin tilted, a defiant gleam in her eye, she spoke loudly enough to include everyone in the room. 'I've decided we should have a change of plan. Both your family and mine will dine together tonight.'

She had to be kidding. Did she really want to subject her mother and father to a dinner where his father and Luis would constantly quarrel and Ivo be so detached he may as well be back in Lucerne training for whatever regatta that was currently preoccupying him? Not to mention his own plans for the evening. 'I'm not available.'

Her eyes narrowed even more at his words. 'I've already organised for a private room in the yacht club for myself, Edwin and Ivo to have dinner and drinks,' Luis protested.

Kara whirled around. 'Well, ring and cancel. We're having a family dinner.' And with that she moved towards the door, saying she would go and find Ricardo on her way to check on her parents, who were both staying in the palace tonight in advance of tomorrow's ceremony, to inform him of the change of plan. Before she left the room she glanced in his direction, her arched eyebrows and challenging stare silently reminding him of her earlier accusation that he was hurtling towards being an isolated grump. *Dio!* She really wasn't going to give him an easy time over this. Well, tough. He knew what he was doing. He needed to keep his distance from her. It was for her own protection. He just couldn't tell her that.

His Highness soon followed her, muttering that he had been planning on having a quiet night alone.

Only Princess Maria seemed pleased. Clapping her hands, she exclaimed, 'I'm looking forward to having Kara in the family—it's about time you men were whipped into shape!'

CHAPTER FIVE

A RAP ON her bedroom door had Kara quickly applying her lipstick, spraying on some perfume, standing from the dressing-table stool to make sure her wrap-around dress wasn't revealing anything it shouldn't be, and sitting back down.

Twisting her loose hair behind her shoulders and picking up her mascara bottle, she said, 'Come in.'

Pushing the door open, Edwin propped a shoulder against the door frame and studied her reflection in the Art Deco dressing table's mirror. Pretending to be applying some mascara, Kara waited for him to speak…while trying not to poke herself in the eye.

Would he stop staring at her? And what was with the dark mood?

Wearing a pale blue shirt over navy trousers, he angled his long body as though to deliberately blockade the entire door. 'It's considered bad luck for the bride and groom to see each other the night before the wedding.'

Picking up her hairbrush, she tried to ignore just how deflated she felt that once again he was preferring to spend time anywhere but in her company. 'I think a special dispensation can be awarded to us, considering our circumstances and the fleeting amount of time we've spent together over the past month.'

Moving across the room, Edwin came to a stand behind her, his bulk filling the delicate dressing-table mirror. A wave of awareness spread up her spine. She shifted forward on her seat.

'You're still angry I went and got your mum?'

Kara lifted one shoulder up and then the other, their separate movements indicative of her mixed feelings on Susan's arrival. At least now there wouldn't be endless speculation on her absence, and it just felt right to have her here. But how she wished that she had come of her own volition…and that Edwin hadn't persuaded her by pointing out the fact that this particular bride would need her mum even more than any other bride because of the fallout that was invariably on the cards for this unconventional marriage that would test even the best of relationships. A fallout that was steamrolling towards them at a faster, more intense rate than

Kara had ever thought possible when she had agreed to the marriage, thanks to Edwin's continuing disappearing acts and avoidance of all things personal. 'Why don't you want to have dinner with us tonight?'

'As I said earlier, I have other plans.'

She ducked her head to catch his gaze, her heart in her mouth, the horror of his elusive answer stripping away any final pretence of being indifferent to his behaviour. 'A woman?' Nick had never been unfaithful but had subtly, and never favourably, compared her to his past girlfriends and work colleagues. It had seriously rattled her trust that men didn't have wandering eyes.

He rocked back on his heels and came to stand to the side of the dressing table, his eyes ablaze. 'Seriously?'

He was furious. For a moment she felt compelled to apologise but then anger rose in her— it was his evasiveness that was driving these questions and she sure as hell was not going to back down. 'Well, what, then?'

His mouth tightened.

Kara smoothed her hand against her hair, certain it was lifting because of the static tension filling the room.

His eyes narrowed as they honed in on her hand. 'Where's your engagement ring?'

Kara pulled open one of the two walnut inlaid drawers on the top of the table and pulled out her ring. 'I take it off when I'm showering.'

He watched her pull it on.

She grimaced at its weight.

'Don't you like it?'

She studied the sapphire. How could she feel nothing for something so beautiful?

Raising her gaze, she studied the man she was about to marry and answered, 'You're not the only one struggling at the idea of marrying, you know.'

With a sigh Edwin dropped to his haunches beside her. 'There is no other woman. I might be struggling with the whole concept of marrying and how on earth to be an even half-decent husband, but there's no other person in this world I'd rather marry. Please believe me on that.' His serious expression gave way to a light smile, his eyes scanning her for a reaction like a lighthouse beam scanning the oceans.

Well, prove just how important I am...spend time with me. Remind me of all the reasons why I agreed to this in the first place.

She eyed him, her poorly constructed defences crumbling in the face of his now keen attention, at the way his shirt pulled tight across his chest, at the smile on his face inviting her to believe in him, to forgive him.

Am I being too needy? Has Nick's stifling devotion warped my understanding as to what a relationship should look like? Am I expecting too much?

'It's not going to be easy dealing with my mum and dad—they're both acting like stressed-out quarrelling Tasmanian devils.'

His mouth quivered.

She crossed her arms. 'What?'

He raised his hands defensively. 'Nothing.'

'Well, they are—at the garden party they refused to be photographed together and matters didn't improve when they found out their luggage had been brought to the same bedroom in the apartment they're sharing.'

Standing with a sigh, he said, 'I'm sorry—that should never have happened.'

'It's okay. The apartment has two other bedrooms. My dad moved into one.'

'I'll organise for another apartment to be allocated to him.'

'I suggested that but they both agreed it would be useful to have someone to navigate the palace with. They're both so anxious and intimidated by everything this weekend. I need your help with dealing with them—that's why I suggested we all have dinner together.'

'Maybe you should have left my family out

of the mix—they're all like a powder keg waiting to go off.'

She stood and reminded him, 'It was you who had said you wanted for you all to be closer as a family.'

He rolled his eyes and shifted away towards the doorway. 'Sometimes I don't think things through enough.'

'Like our marriage?'

He came to a stop in the centre of the room. 'Not that…' he paused his gaze sweeping down over her '…but I shouldn't.' Again he hesitated, his gaze settling on her mouth. Reaching down, he plucked her silver and gold sandals from where she had earlier placed them on one of the two gilt stools sitting at the base of her bed. Well, her bed for now. Tomorrow her items would be moved to Edwin's bedroom next door.

Passing the sandals to her, he said in a rush, 'We'd better go down for dinner.'

Kara grabbed her sandals. Right, she'd had enough. Skirting around Edwin, she darted across the room and, banging the door shut, she leant against it with all of her weight. 'Right, we're sorting this out now once and for all. What is going on? Why are you shutting me out?'

Edwin moved across the room and, standing in front of her, placed his hand on the door handle and twisted it. 'Let's go—my father is going to be livid if I'm late again today.'

She pushed her weight even harder against the door. 'Not until we discuss this.'

He snapped his hand off the door handle. 'Fine. Give me some examples.'

'Today you arrived late for the garden party—'

'I was collecting your mother—'

'Why leave it till the day before the wedding? And this afternoon at the party, not once did you come to my side. What groom does that? It was embarrassing. And tonight you have some mysterious plans you're refusing to talk about.'

'You know how much I have to deal with right now, with the succession and persuading that German bank to locate here, not to mention all of the changes to the government structures I want to hammer out in advance of my enthronement.'

'There's nothing in that list that would stop you actually talking to me.'

God, how was she going to get through to him?

The urge to touch him, to be close to him once again, had her reach out her index finger to give a single light tap to his temple. 'I have no idea what's going on in there,' a tightness in her throat replacing the burn of anger in her belly, she tapped her finger against his chest, 'or in your heart.'

For a moment his shoulders flexed tight as though he was about to leap away from her. But then they dropped and, bowing his head, he stood silently in front of her. His hair was damp. Citrus mingled with his usual clean woody scent. She pushed herself even tighter against the door, her shoulder blades digging into the wood, for fear of giving in to the temptation of running her hands through the damp silkiness of his hair or cupping her hand against the vulnerable strength of his neck or, most compelling of all, the pull to move towards him and take shelter against his body.

Bruised golden eyes met hers. 'You deserve to have your mother here at your wedding. I wanted to make you happy. That's the only reason why I went and brought her here. But I obviously made a mistake.'

She closed her eyes against the softness of his voice. 'What would make me happy is if we could go back to how we were before all of this—where has our friendship disappeared to?'

She opened her eyes on his sigh.

He shifted to stand squarely in front of her.

Bare inches separating them, he studied her for long moments, a denseness entering the air between them. 'I'm struggling...'

His eyes shifted down to her lips.

Pinpricks of temptation tingled across her skin.

Her hips snaked outwards towards him. She slammed them back against the door, her tailbone colliding with the wood, making her already unsteady legs tremble.

His head tilted, his eyes remaining fixed on her mouth as though it was a complex problem he was trying to understand.

With a distracted air, he repeated in another whisper, 'I'm struggling,' again he paused, and then his head lifted and his eyes blazed into hers.

Unable to breathe, unable to look away from the intensity of his gaze, hormones washing through her body like a lethal overdose, Kara felt her heart cry out for him to say something, something that would make everything okay, that would destroy the fear inside of her.

'I'm struggling...' he blinked and blinked again and, just like that, the passion, the hunger in his eyes was gone, traded for a wary defensiveness '... I'm struggling with the idea of being a husband.'

The feeling of being robbed of something she didn't even understand had her duck away from him and move into the centre of the room.

'Well, you'd better get used to it because this time tomorrow you'll be my husband—if you still want to go through with it.'

'Don't you?'

How many times had she asked herself that question over the past few weeks, her heart and instinct warning her to tread carefully? But her pride, her need to stick to her word and promises, seeing already the benefit her new position was bringing to Young Adults Together, her desire to help Edwin despite his recent infuriating behaviour, all had her want to see this through. 'On a number of conditions.'

She ignored Edwin's grimace and, holding up her hand counted off with her fingers, 'First condition is that we're going to have breakfast together every morning from now on. Second, we are trekking in the mountains and watching a movie together at least once a week. Third, you promised me a nice honeymoon. I'll accept your schedule is too crazy to allow for one right now, but at some point in this two years of marriage, I expect a holiday, and a spectacular one at that.'

Throwing his hands in the air, Edwin answered, 'Fine.' Opening the door, he added, 'Now can we please go to dinner?'

Coming to a stop where he was standing holding the door open for her, she attempted to hide just how vulnerable she was feeling inside with even more bravado. 'It's not too late to pull out of the wedding, you know—I won't take it personally.'

He smiled at that. His hand lightly touched her forearm. 'Getting married is way more complex than I ever anticipated...' he tilted his head, the tenderness in his eyes melting her heart '... but you're still the only person in the world for me.'

Their main course finished, Edwin caught her eye from the opposite side of the dining table and, looking in the direction of his father and her mother, who were seated to her right, he raised an eyebrow. Kara smiled. Who would have predicted his father and her mother would bond over a shared passion for olives?

Her mother lived alone in a two-bedroom *cortijo*, surrounded by olive groves, in the hills north of Málaga City. Throughout the meal she had described in vivid detail her new life tending to her olive trees, talking about her hopes and fears for this season's harvest. For the first time in years her mother was talking about the future.

The waiting staff reappeared, all five of them in a gracefully coordinated dance placing a tiny but exquisitely formed trio of chocolate desserts before each diner.

As they backed out of the room, her dad stood up.

Kara held her breath. Her poor father's hands

were trembling so badly the red wine in his glass was sloshing about.

He directed his attention towards Edwin's father. 'I would like to thank you for your welcome and hospitality, Your Highness.'

He raised his glass even higher, and the rest of the people at the table reached for their glasses to join in with the toast, but her dad wasn't finished.

Clearing his throat loudly, he added, 'I ask that you and your family take good care of my...' his voice cracked and it took him a few seconds to add, 'my little girl.'

Little girl. God, it was corny and sentimental but she could not help the feeling of delight and belonging that filled her heart at her dad's description. For so many years she had believed he had forgotten that—that she was his daughter, that she was the same person he'd given piggy-back rides to around their garden, jumping over sweeping brushes, pretending they were taking part in the Cheltenham Gold Cup.

She waited for her father to look in her direction, but instead his focus remained on Edwin's father. He was waiting for a response. He had thrown down a gauntlet. Her dad, a small-time builder, was challenging the sovereign of a small but powerful country. Kara wanted to burst with pride.

His Highness's frown deepened to a bottomless ravine transecting his forehead. Kara swallowed. He had done nothing in the weeks since their engagement to indicate he was shedding any of his misgivings as to Edwin's choice of bride.

Sitting back in his chair, he studied her father, then her mother and then finally her, taking his time, a monarch accustomed to people waiting for his considered judgement. Her palms started to sweat.

Edwin said, 'You have our word—'

With an annoyed shake of his head, His Highness interrupted Edwin, his attention now fully on his eldest son. 'My marriage was arranged.' He stopped and chuckled. Kara gave a nervous smile, uncertain what direction this conversation was going in. 'At first my wife and I argued. She actually said I was too arrogant and had to accept that the marriage was one of equals. Of course, she was right, and after a while we became friends. And with time we grew to love one another.' His gaze shifting towards her, he added, 'From the most inauspicious starts, miracles can happen.'

What did he mean by that?

Edwin's father did not wait for her to work that question out. Instead he stood and raised his glass in salute to her father, who was still standing and waiting for a response to his question. 'I will give you my word that we will take care of your daughter as long as she's a member of our family.'

Her father frowned. Kara reddened.

Shooting out of his seat, Edwin raised his own glass, his expression pinched. 'Please be assured, Mr Duffy, that we will take care of Kara *always*.'

Her father's gaze moved from Edwin to his father and back again before he said quietly, 'Thank you, Edwin,' and then took his seat.

Edwin remained standing. He rolled his shoulders and raised his wine glass again. 'To my mother and Michael. We miss you dearly but you will live on for ever in our memories and actions.'

A tangle of emotions lodged in her throat at Edwin's softly spoken and unexpected words. The entire table just stared at him, nobody raising their glasses. A twitch began to beat in Edwin's cheek.

Her mother stood up.

Oh, God, was she about to walk out of the room at the mention of Michael's name?

Raising her glass, her mother waited with a quiet dignity and slowly the rest of the table rose to join her. Only then did she say, 'To Princess Cristina and Michael.'

They all sat down. They had no sooner done so when His Highness added, raising his glass again, 'And here's to many grandchildren in the future.'

Edwin sighed.

Her parents stared open-mouthed at His Highness.

Her mother was the first to gather herself enough to splutter, 'I really don't think so.' Sending a glare in her and Edwin's direction, she added, 'Please tell me you aren't going to be so foolish as to bring a child into this?'

'Of course not,' Kara answered.

In a disgruntled tone, Edwin's father demanded, 'Why ever not?'

Her mother huffed. 'I am not having my daughter left to raise a child on her own.'

Princess Maria, who was seated next to her father, asked with a bewildered expression, 'Why would Kara raise a child on her own?'

'Exactly my question,' His Highness added, staring in Edwin's direction.

Luis gave a cynical laugh and asked his father, 'Are you happy with the mess you've caused?'

'You never specified I have to marry for ever,' Edwin pointed out, lifting his wine glass to his mouth but then lowering it to the table, not having taken a drink from it. He pushed it away from him as though irritated by the golden-hued wine.

Princess Maria gasped. 'Are you saying—?'

His Highness interrupted with a flick of his hand, 'Of course this is a marriage of convenience. Did you really think Edwin had changed his opinion on ever committing himself to a relationship? I had no choice but to force his hand. This country needs successors. This family needs a new generation.'

With a horrified expression, Princess Maria asked her brother, 'Have you lost all sense?'

His Highness grimaced, but then sat back in his chair, a smile forming on his lips. He glanced in her direction and then Edwin's.

A queasy feeling formed in her belly.

'You saw the engagement photos for yourself. Are you seriously telling me that I was wrong in pushing Edwin to make a choice in his bride?' Edwin's father demanded.

Across the table, her father, red in the face, growled, 'Can I remind you that they are divorcing in two years' time?'

His Highness blanched. And then, leaning forward, he yelled at Edwin, 'Two years? Are you serious? Two years is nothing. You're not even prepared to give the marriage a chance.'

That twitch in his cheek now on overdrive, Edwin answered with poorly disguised fury,

'You do not have a say in this.' With that he stood and muttered, 'I need some air.'

Kara stood and followed him.

Edwin's father called out, 'You can't divorce. We've never had a divorce in this family and we're not having one now.'

CHAPTER SIX

IN THE FAST approaching twilight, a figure ran out onto the road. Slamming on the brakes, Edwin cursed, his motorbike skidding on the gravel surface. The figure, about to be pelted with incoming stones, leapt out of the way.

Tugging off his helmet, he muttered a low curse. Kara was barefoot, her sandals in her hand, her dress, a fine layer of gold and yellow silk material, skimming over the gentle curves of her body. Thoughts on Kara's body, no matter how delectable they were, were not where his focus needed to be right now. 'Being mowed down by a motorbike is a drastic way to get out of our wedding tomorrow.'

She stepped off the grass verge. 'I'm coming with you.'

He pulled on his helmet. 'Stay with your parents. I'm sure they have plenty of things to discuss with you after that get-together.'

Oh, for crying out loud.

Kara went to get on behind him. He reached out to stop her but she slapped his hand away and climbed on. Muttering, he turned the motorbike back in the direction of the palace's garage.

Inside the garage, which had once been part of the palace's own flour mill, he climbed off. And waited for Kara to follow. But instead she sat there and pretended to ignore him.

He walked out of the garage.

Kara chased after him.

He followed the path towards the pool house and then made a quick divert away towards the sea. Still Kara followed him. 'Are you going to follow me all night?'

'Yes, until you at least tell me where you were going.'

Okay, so he was acting crazily. This was not the behaviour of a grown man, never mind one about to succeed to the throne. But his head was about to explode *and* there was no way he could be around Kara right now. 'Look, I want some time alone—is that too much to ask?'

Gesturing in the direction of the palace, she said, 'Well, you're certainly not leaving me here to face *that* lot alone.' Popping a hand on her hip she added, 'And actually, yes, it *is* too much for you to ask of your fiancée. You should want to be with me.'

Want to be with her…that was the problem:

he wanted to be with her, but for all the wrong reasons. And it was eating him up inside. 'What do you want from me?'

Her mouth set hard, her eyes blazing, she answered, 'To not wreck our friendship. We need to talk. Properly. We can't keep burying our heads in the sand and pretending that marrying, your succession, the craziness that's going on around us isn't impacting on us as individuals but also as a couple.' Then with an exasperated gesture with her hands she added, 'At least Nick blew hot and cold…right now you're just blowing cold constantly.'

For long moments she stared at him defiantly but then her mouth wobbled and she blinked hard. His heart sank. There were tears in her eyes. 'I'm really messing up here, aren't I?'

'I can't survive the next two years if you're going to be this remote. I need your friendship, your support. I need to understand what's going on inside your head,' on a sigh her shoulders lifted, her eyes sad pools of blue, 'because when I don't I feel so sad and lonely. And I didn't sign up for those things. And I know you didn't either.'

He wasn't sad or lonely. Was he?

An uneasiness spread through his bones, bringing a pressing need to end this conversation. But how was he supposed to walk away from those bruised blue eyes holding him to account?

His throat tightened when he realised what it was he needed to do. He had to stop running away into the safety of his own thoughts and isolation. He had to give Kara what she needed and deserved from him. Yes, it might mess with his head, make him deeply uncomfortable and frustrated, but that was his problem, not Kara's. 'I was going for a bike ride into the mountains to clear my head. And, given that you previously said you'd never ride with me again, I assumed you wouldn't want to come.'

She bit back a grin, rightly knowing he was giving in to her. 'I'll try not to scream this time.'

Back in the garage he gave Kara the smallest bike leathers he could find, probably a relic from the time Luis was a mountain-bike fanatic, much to his father's disapproval. For the teenage Luis, the faster and more dangerous the sport, the better.

Then he searched out a suitable-size helmet and boots. He waited outside the garage while Kara pulled on all of the gear.

She emerged a sensual mix of silk and leather. He grinned. 'Great look.' He ducked his head, pretending to be checking the hand clutch. His comment had been supposed to come out as a tease but instead had sounded way too familiar and suggestively carnal. He fired up the engine, trying to ignore the blush on Kara's cheeks.

He drove out of the palace and through the narrow streets of Monrosa City before they began their long climb up into the mountains, the road a series of endless hairpin turns. The sky was rapidly turning from a pink breath of fire to inky blackness. There was little traffic out at this time of the evening, so he was able to drive hard, needing the surge of the breeze against his skin to counterbalance the sweet warmth of Kara's body behind him.

After half an hour they reached their destination. The viewpoint was set high up in the mountain, allowing a clear view of Monrosa City below them. On a headland to the east, the San Gabriel lighthouse flickered.

Kara removed her helmet and threw her head backwards. 'Wow, so many stars.'

Leading her away through the forest, using a torch to guide their way, he brought her to the opposite side of the mountain to a clearing with picnic tables. She gasped and turned around in a slow circle, her neck stretched back to take in the endless night sky that hung over them like a glittering dark blanket just out of their reach.

'It's stunning.'

'There's no light pollution on this side of the mountain. Locally this area is called Angels'

Reach. People say it's the closest point to heaven on the island.'

Balancing against the edge of a picnic table, Kara asked, 'It's a special place for you?'

'It used to be, when I was younger.'

'And now?'

Now he wasn't certain what he felt for Angels' Reach. He hadn't visited the mountain for years. 'Are you certain it's not bad luck to see each other the night before the wedding?'

Kara studied him for a moment. 'I'm not sure you can bring bad luck to a marriage of convenience.' She gave a light laugh. 'It's not as though we have to worry about falling out of love or anything like that.'

Silence stretched out between them. Kara tilted her head again to stargaze, eventually asking in a soft voice, 'Is this where you had been planning to visit before I stopped you?'

'Yes.'

'Why here?'

'I like the view. And, as I said, I needed space to think.'

She raised an eyebrow. 'And you couldn't find some space to think in a seventy-room palace?'

He scuffed his boot along the dry earth, remembering what it was like to lie down on it and hear his mother whisper tales from the folklore of her native Aragon. 'I should have brought something for us to drink.'

'You're shutting me out again.'

He started at the anger in her voice. Exasperation, frustration at his own avoidance, his inability to articulate the feelings that were tightly sewn into the fabric of his being and Kara's impossible desire for him to unpick those feelings thread by thread had him respond just as angrily, 'I don't know how to let you in.'

She turned away from him. Went and sat on the bench of the picnic table and stared out into the darkness in the direction of the Mediterranean that the waning crescent moon did little to illuminate.

He went and sat beside her.

She shuffled away, leaning back against the tabletop. Waves of irritation pulsated in his direction. 'Start with the small things—it doesn't have to be anything profound. Tell me about the first time you came here, for instance.'

He tossed the flashlight between his hands, a jittery energy entering his bloodstream. 'I can't remember the first time—it was decades ago.'

Those waves of irritation from her moved across to him in even quicker pulses.

Dio, this was so hard. Why did he find it near impossible to speak? Why did it feel like torture?

'My mother used to bring me here to celebrate my birthday. We'd sneak out before midnight and we'd sit here counting down the minutes until it was my birthday.' Something caught in his throat, but he could tell that Kara expected more, so he forced himself to find the words that described memories he had deliberately ignored for years. 'She used to say that she wanted to be the first to whisper *happy birthday* to me.'

Kara sighed. And whispered, 'She sounds wonderful.'

Something large and significant twisted in his chest at the soft wistfulness, the respect in Kara's voice. He held her gaze, his heart tumbling, tumbling, tumbling again and again and again at not just the understanding in her eyes but also the eagerness there, the eagerness to know more about his mother. 'Yes, she was.'

'Tell me more.'

An image of his mother, down on all fours on the palace lawn, chasing after him and his two brothers, pretending to be a grizzly bear, had him smile. 'She was playful, constantly thinking up new things for us all to do, new adventures for us to undertake. One summer we created our own pirate island on the palace's private beach—we even made our own lookout tower using old wine barrels she found in the cellar. And she used to dream up ways to trick the media into not following us, which of course was like something out of a spy movie for us.' He rolled his shoulders, his heart clogged with emotions he didn't want to have to process. 'It's hard to describe but somehow she just managed to make me feel secure, certain about the world.'

Kara twisted towards him. 'You wanted to remember your mum tonight.'

He shrugged.

'I'm sorry she's not going to be there tomorrow.'

A fissure opened up in his heart. 'Me too.'

'I'm sure she wouldn't be impressed with your dad forcing you into a marriage of convenience.'

He laughed at that, imagining his mother's reaction. 'She would have gone crazy.' Then, catching Kara's eye, he admitted, 'But she'd have liked you.'

Kara gave a snort. 'I'm sure she'd have wanted a more suitable bride for you, someone who understands royal protocol and doesn't constantly ruffle feathers, which I seem to be making my speciality.' She let out a sigh. 'Victor isn't happy that I'm refusing to back down on my tour of Europe to raise awareness for Young Adults Together. He wants me to dedicate more time to attending events with you instead. And the chamberlain is putting every obstacle possible in the way of my plans to open up parts of the palace to the public. And as for my proposal to start an apprenticeship programme within the palace for disadvantaged young school leavers... I've never heard so many reasons as to why something won't work. I get that there's a tradition of roles being passed within families—but nepotism like that is just plain unfair.'

He grinned and bumped his shoulder against hers playfully. 'Please don't stop questioning everything. The household needs a shake-up and you're also taking the heat off me.'

Kara pursed her lips and eyed him suspiciously. 'Are you saying I'm your fall guy?'

Did she really have to draw his attention to her mouth like that? It wasn't as though he was ignoring it in the first place. And why was he so damn distracted by her knee touching his thigh?

Her leather jacket was moulded to her curves like a second skin, its zip hanging just at the valley of her breasts like an agent provocateur. Blood pumping through him in hard beats, he placed an arm behind her back. 'Never a guy.'

Her eyes widened. She gave him an uncertain smile.

His hand touched her arm.

She jumped but then settled, leaning ever so slightly towards him, allowing his fingers to curl even more around the soft leather of her jacket. Soft leather. Soft lips. Soft skin.

Silence, darkness, unfinished business.

He eased her closer. She didn't resist.

Her loose hair tickled the back of his hand.

Memories of her scent, floral with an undertone of something earthier, wiped out the forest scent surrounding them.

Her shoulder slotted under his arm, the softness of her body pressed close to where his heart was hammering.

He touched a finger to her chin, tilting her head so that their gazes married. He breathed deep at the heat in her eyes, the parting of her lips. He inched towards her mouth, all thought wiped out by pure physical need. Their lips touched, her mouth even more sensual and lush than before. He tried to hold himself back but that lasted all of five seconds before he was deepening the kiss, wanting to taste, inhale every part of her.

And her hand on his neck pulled him even deeper into the kiss.

Kara was moving.

Panicked, he jerked away, worried he had read this all wrong and Kara was trying to get away.

She pulled him back, her bottom landing on his lap. He chuckled into their kiss and he could feel her lips draw up into a smile. But they didn't stop.

He pulled her hip in against his belly, fire raging through him, her hands raking through his hair.

He fumbled for the zip of her jacket and lowered it, his thumb tracing down over the smooth skin of her breasts.

He groaned again. Her bottom wriggled on his lap.

He wanted to part the material of her dress, expose the lace bra he could feel beneath the silk. He wanted to twist her fully towards him and have her wrap her legs around his waist. He eased away, his head swimming with crazy, destructive thoughts.

But only seconds after he broke their kiss, less than an inch away from her, with a sound of protest she pulled him back, both hands clasping his neck.

Burning, urgent, unthinking need yelled at him to stay there. To lose himself in her. But he had to stop. Before the mess of their impending marriage became an even more tangled chaos of emotions.

He unclasped her hands. Drew back from her mouth.

She stared into his eyes, dazed.

And then with a sound of disbelief she flew

off his lap, gawked at him and rocked on her heels before collapsing back down on the bench.

She yanked her jacket zip back up, clamping the skirt of her dress between her legs. 'I hope there's no paparazzi with night-vision cameras hiding in the woods.'

He laughed, glad she was making light of the frenetic intensity of what had just happened.

'Our kisses...they're kind of confusing, aren't they?' she said quietly.

His laughter died. He had no way of explaining them other than as the result of human desire. 'I guess we're both young and healthy and it's been a while since either of us were in a relationship.'

She nodded eagerly. 'And the craziness of our situation isn't helping—maybe subconsciously we think we should be finding each other attractive.' She stopped, her expression growing horrified. 'Not that I'm saying you find me attractive—'

He interrupted her, 'I think we can at least admit to each other the chemistry between us.'

Did she really think their subconscious could be fooling them to that extent? But who was he to argue? If she was happy to believe that, then so was he.

'So what do we do about this attraction?'

Her brow furrowed. 'I don't know. Not beat

ourselves up too much when it happens, I guess. And, more importantly, not ascribe too much significance to it…the survival of our friendship is what's important.'

He inhaled deeply. 'I don't ever want to hurt you.'

She nodded. 'I guess it's down to both of us individually to keep everything in perspective—to remember that this is a marriage of convenience thrust upon two people who have no interest in marrying and no desire to marry.'

He pulled his heel along the soft earth, a deep channel forming in its wake. 'Before Nick, did you see yourself marrying?'

She shrugged and scrunched her nose in thought. 'What happened with my parents put me off…but Nick definitely put a solid nail in the coffin of love and marriage for me.' She gave a light shiver. 'I struggle with the idea of trusting someone enough to commit myself to them for ever. I'd hate the vulnerability of that. I'd constantly be watching for a time when they'd try to manipulate me, hurt me. And that's not fair, is it?' Pausing, she considered him. 'You know what, you've never really given me a good reason why you're not interested in marriage?'

He flattened the channel of earth with the sole of his shoe. 'I like my own company. I don't think I'm husband material—I prefer to give my energy to my work.' Then, standing up, he held out his hand to her. 'I'd better get you home.'

She looked at his hand and then looked him straight in the eye. 'Being single suits some people…but only if it's for the right reasons.' Then, standing up too, she tugged him towards the wooden barrier at the edge of the picnic area. 'I think I can hear the sea.'

He leant forward, twisting his head. 'I think I can too. I've never heard it before, even in all the times I came here with my mother.'

She smiled at him, her hand touching his cheek. 'Thank you for bringing me here, for telling me about your mum. It's good to know you better.'

It did feel good to have spoken about his mother. He smiled at how Kara's eyes were dancing with pleasure, a connection, a spark, a sense of place making him intensely happy. But then, just as quickly as that happiness arrived, it disappeared, the intimacy of the moment making him uneasy. Was he making himself vulnerable by being this open? Was he setting them up for a whole load of heartache when this marriage ended by their being too close to one another?

CHAPTER SEVEN

MONICA, THE PALACE'S head florist, moved from table to table, adjusting a fraction the elaborate floral arrangements sitting in tall, clear vases at the centre of every table in the ballroom.

On seeing him, she went to leave, but Edwin gestured for her to stay and finish her work.

The doors out to the terrace were opened back, the heat of the day drifting into the coolness of the room.

Beyond the terrace, on the shimmering water, boats in full sail glided through the rolling white-topped waves.

In two hours he would be married. A husband.

He turned away from the golden dome of the cathedral.

The ballroom was a reflection of the view across the harbour. The vast gold chandeliers towering over the tables laden down with gold cutlery and gold-rimmed plates bearing the royal crest mirrored the cathedral's dome, the olive branches in the floral arrangements the green and silver glimmer of the Mediterranean, the pink blush roses the narrow buildings of the old town.

Ricardo bustled into the room. Did a double-take when he spotted Edwin.

'Is everything okay, Your Highness?'

He nodded. 'I want to ensure everything is in place for the wedding meal later.' From the moment he had woken this morning he had been feeling off balance. Tetchy and nervous, with a side dollop of a tightness in his throat. Was he coming down with something?

Last night, talking beneath the stars, kissing…it had all felt too good, too exhilarating. He hadn't dated for close to two years. No wonder kissing Kara was igniting a fire inside him.

He needed to get through today. Not overthink it. Which was why he was here, unnecessarily inspecting the ballroom like a nervous housekeeper. Anything to distract him. Kara had left their apartment early this morning, as arranged, to get ready for the ceremony in her parents' apartment. Unable to stomach breakfast, he had paced the apartment, ready for the ceremony way too early, and even he couldn't bring himself to work on his wedding day.

Ricardo cleared his throat. 'Is everything to your satisfaction?'

Eucalyptus leaves wound their way up all seven layers of their wedding cake. On top two simple figures crafted from wood stood beneath an arch of intertwined leaves. Kara had asked him if he wanted an input into the cake. He hadn't. The tightness in his throat intensified. The cake perfectly symbolised their treks into the mountains of Monrosa. He turned to Ricardo. 'Everything is perfect.'

Relief washed over Ricardo's expression. 'We want to ensure you and Miss Duffy have a wonderful wedding day. We're all so happy for you. Miss Duffy has been very supportive in the preparations and it will be a pleasure to work for her in the coming years.'

Behind Ricardo, Luis walked into the room and chuckled. 'I'm sure Kara will be a dream to work for in comparison to our father.'

Ricardo flinched, made a non-committal sound and fled from the room.

Edwin sighed. 'There was no need for that.'

Luis shrugged. 'We've been looking everywhere for you. It's time to go.'

Ivo and his father were waiting for them on the central steps out in the courtyard. Ivo was dressed in the same navy-blue officer dress uniform of the Monrosian army as Luis, their father in the red dress uniform of the Commander of the Forces. Today he was wearing the black officer tunic of the Marines, gold cuffs on the sleeves, gold braiding on the shoulders. Across the tunic he wore the red and white sash representing the Order of St Philip, and pinned to the fabric the gold insignia of the two other Monrosian orders.

Without preamble they lined up, equidistantly apart. Edwin stood in the centre beside his father, Ivo to his right, Luis to his father's left.

At the western apartments, horses and carriages were awaiting Kara and her entourage. He closed his eyes, a wave of gratitude, of affection, of respect for her making him dizzy. How many friends would agree to something this enormous, this public, this life-altering? He *had* to make this marriage work.

With a call from their commander, the twelve soldiers flanking them on either side, all in their Sixth Infantry khaki uniforms, led them towards the closed fifteenth-century wooden gates that led out onto the cobbled streets of the city.

It took four of the household guard to open the gates.

A wave of sound rolled towards them. The waiting crowd cheered and waved their purple and gold Monrosa flags, aided by the warm summer breeze.

The clamour, the close scrutiny, the fevered elation of the crowd sent a sickening sensation through him but he continued to walk at the steady beat that had been drilled into him from the moment he could walk, falling in behind the rest of the Sixth Infantry regiment already waiting outside the palace walls, the Second Regiment falling in behind them.

They walked down the incline that would take them to the narrow streets of the old town and then on to the harbour front towards Monrosa Cathedral, the cheering swelling.

He clenched his hands, the happy calls so at odds with the low weeping and murmuring that had accompanied them the last time they had marched together to the cathedral.

That time, with every step he had taken, his frustration with his father had inched ever higher. Why had he forced them to walk through the crowds to their mother's funeral? Why had he thought it was the duty of three bereaved children to march, just so the public would have the opportunity to express their grief at the passing of their beloved Princess Cristina?

The morning of the funeral, he had held Ivo in his arms and had promised that he would not be forced to march. But, despite his arguing fiercely with his father, his father had refused to relent, forcing Ivo to join them.

That was the day they had lost Ivo to his own impenetrable thoughts.

For his part, Edwin had been so full of anger and disbelief that he soon realised that to survive he would have to detach himself. Shut down all his emotions. Not react when his father had angrily demanded to know why he and Luis had refused to accompany their mother when she had gone out riding that day with Ivo. Not admit his own anger towards Ivo for insisting they go riding even though their mother had complained of vertigo earlier that day.

Now they swept through Plaza Nueva, the thunderous applause startling pigeons from the roof of the Tufail Observatory Tower. A dark-haired girl of five or six, perched on her father's shoulders, waved a cut-out of him and Kara on their engagement day. He smiled at her. She dropped the cut-out, her eyes wide, her mouth a perfect circle of surprise.

His mother would have loved every moment of this. She wouldn't have even tried to hide her pride in her husband and three sons' marching together as one seemingly united family.

How they had all failed her.

They turned a sharp right, the open harbour bringing a strong sea breeze and the sight of waves lapping against the quay walls. People hung from the upstairs windows of the quayside cafes, filming the procession on their phones.

A girl called out her love for Luis. His father sighed loudly.

At Plaza Santa Ana, the Cardinal of Monrosa was waiting for them on the cathedral steps.

Inside came welcome near silence apart from the low whispering from the already assembled guests. Edwin's nose twitched thanks to the heavy scent of incense.

He was about to follow the cardinal when his father placed a hand on his arm. 'You can make this work if you want to.'

He bit back the temptation to laugh.

Did his father seriously think this forced marriage, already fraying at the edges, could be made to work just to serve his egotistical desire to ensure a future heir?

He walked away, smiled and nodded his way down the aisle, the beaming grins of Kara's family, friends and colleagues punching him in the stomach. How many lies had she had to tell on his behalf?

He took a seat at the top pew.

Tried to breathe.

His mother's casket had sat only feet away from where he sat now.

He had refused to look at it. Instead he had tilted his head and tried to count the number of flowers on the triptych of stained-glass windows behind the altar. But the disbelief kept dragging him back—to the fact that only four days prior his mother had left to take Ivo horse-riding. He and Luis had been supposed to go too but they had become caught up in a battle to win a game of tennis and had refused to leave. He had vaguely waved his mother goodbye. Hadn't replied to her departing call to be kind to one another. Her horse had startled and thrown her off, causing a catastrophic head injury.

Ivo, alone on the isolated trail they had been following within the palace grounds, had raised the alarm on her mobile phone and had frantically carried out the emergency services' instructions on how to help her, a ten-year-old child, alone, carrying the responsibility for saving his mother.

Losing her had destroyed them.

He placed his hands on his knees. Light-headed.

Time stretched out. His father grumbled at Kara's lateness.

Kara was going to walk down the aisle, wasn't she? What if she had changed her mind?

His heart boomed in his chest. Only one person, since his mother had died, had settled him—Kara. Her acceptance of him as well as astute challenges to his ways of thinking and behaving, her energy, had freed him.

Dammit, where was she?

Cold terror ran through his veins.

Had he blown it? Had he thrown away their friendship for this farce?

Standing at the bottom of the aisle, while Triona and Siza brought her long train under control, her hands resting on both of her parents' arms, Kara felt her legs buckle.

And for a moment a crazy thought passed through her mind at lightning speed.

What if she spoke out? Right here? Right now? Explained that she couldn't be the answer to what the media were terming a new era of optimism in Monrosa? Explained she understood the marriage was creating an unprecedented feel-good factor and was being hailed as an example of hope triumphing after the tragedy of the country losing Princess Cristina, but the media's new near adoration of her, lauding her charity work, describing her relationship with Edwin as the ultimate love story that saw friendship blossom into enduring love, was so far from the truth that she felt as if she was going to burn up in shame?

What if she explained there definitely would be no babies born to them?

What if she made it clear this was only a marriage between friends? One that would end one day, but until that happened she would have Edwin's back and would try her very best to be the princess Monrosa deserved?

What would happen if she said all that, cleared the air?

Chaos probably.

'Are you ready?'

She wanted to say no to her father's question but instead she nodded *yes*. Which was a good thing because there was no way she was going to be heard anyway. The cathedral practically shook as the Bridal Chorus boomed from the pipes of the organ positioned on the gallery overhead, the notes flinging themselves against the vast roof of the even vaster cathedral.

Edwin jerked in his seat, music booming against the stone pillars as the organist began to play. The cardinal and his fellow celebrants on the altar looked down the aisle, a smile transforming each of their up-till-now serious expressions.

Kara had that effect on people.

He shouldn't look back. Not yet.

But he didn't give a damn.

He needed to see her. He needed to see her with a desperation that burned through him and scorched his heart.

He breathed in deeply, stepped even further out into the aisle. Desperate to have her look in his direction, desperate for a connection.

Flanked by her mother and father, her bridesmaids carrying her train, Kara walked towards him, her gaze sweeping to either side of the aisle but not once looking in his direction.

A veil was the only adornment in her tied-up hair. His aunt hadn't persuaded her to wear a tiara after all.

Her full-skirted satin dress with its sweetheart neckline was overlaid with delicate lace that skimmed her shoulders and the length of her arms.

In her hands she carried the same blush-pink roses interlaced with olive and eucalyptus leaves as the displays in the palace ballroom.

There was heat on her cheeks.

She was beautiful.

Look at me.

Her head dipped as though studying the blue and white mosaic tiles on the floor.

Look at me, Kara. Let me know you're okay. I need you...and I don't understand why, but I'm panicking here.

And then finally, only a few steps away, she looked towards him.

Her gaze was heavy with emotion.

His heart pounded.

She gave him a tentative smile.

He blinked away the stinging sensation in his eyes.

She was here.

Standing in the centre of the aisle, powerful, intent, Edwin held her gaze with a burning intensity. Kara's heart turned inside out.

His hair was newly cut. His black, heavily adorned military uniform suited the hard planes of his face, the seriousness and loyalty of his personality.

Her parents peeled away to awkwardly shake Edwin's hand before they took their seats. From the corner of her eye she saw the fond smiles from their guests taking in the fact both her mother and father had guided her down the aisle to their future son-in-law, a family united in their joy of the ceremony about to take place, when the sad reality was that they had only announced this morning that they were both going to escort her down the aisle, united in their ongoing objections to the wedding.

Well, at least they were finally agreeing on something for the first time in a decade.

The music disappeared and silence fell on the cathedral.

This was about to happen. She was about to marry this man. Her best friend, her saviour, the person who kept her sane, who got her, and with whom she had the most uncomplicated relationship in her life—she was about to marry him and step into a very complicated world.

Edwin continued to stare at her.

She smiled, not certain what to do, not certain how to react to his intensity. 'Hi.'

She waited for him to say something in response.

At the altar the cardinal cleared his throat, and made a gesture for them to approach the altar steps, as they had rehearsed.

But Edwin didn't budge.

He leant down and whispered, 'You're here.'

She swayed at the low tenderness of his voice.

He took her hand in his and led her to the altar.

The cardinal smiled but then frowned in the direction of their joined hands. The joining of hands was supposed to come later in the ceremony.

But Edwin's grasp only tightened around her trembling hand.

She needed to pull herself together.

She was *not* going to crash and burn under the pressure of all this expectation. It was messing with her head and distorting her feelings for Edwin, and she needed to get a grip. She had to stop struggling to keep her emotions in check around him, and as for her body—well, that was off in a la-la world of misguided sexual attraction. As was witnessed last night. She would have happily slept with him. Her legs threatened to buckle under her again. But this time it wasn't terror but a lick of heat in her belly, remembering the dominance of his mouth, the sweep of his hand against her breast.

This was so wrong. She shouldn't be having these thoughts standing in front of a cardinal, being watched by millions worldwide.

She needed to hold on to the cold, hard fact that this was nothing more than a theatrical performance. A performance that would allow her to champion the work of Young Adults Together.

She dropped her gaze, a stab of loneliness emptying her lungs. Michael would have understood her reasoning. He would have agreed to subvert an institution like marriage to further a good cause. Wouldn't he?

When it came to the exchanging of vows, vows she had written, agonising over every word, not wanting to publicly commit to anything with which they would never follow through, she held her breath and willed herself to remain detached.

But Edwin's intense golden gaze shredded any hopes of her remaining indifferent.

'I promise you my friendship, loyalty, trust and understanding regardless of the obstacles we may face together.' His voice danced along her spine. She tightened her fingers around his, needing an anchor as she made the same simple vows, praying they would survive all the obstacles that littered their future.

And then the cardinal invited them to kiss.

Edwin touched his fingers to her jawline. Her heart kicked hard at the tenderness of his touch. She was doing it again…confusing acting with reality. She straightened, trying to regain some backbone.

She wished he would stop gazing at her as though she was the love of his life and just kiss her. He didn't need to over-egg this. The guests wouldn't suspect this was anything but a love marriage.

But he stayed there, touching her face, reverently, gently.

People began to shuffle in their seats.

His father muttered something.

This was torture. Unfair. Wrecking her heart.

And, fool that she was, she wished they could stay in this moment for eternity. A moment when the past and future didn't matter.

Something cracked inside of her.

I want closeness and intimacy with you. I want to be my true self. I want the freedom, just for a while, to have my heart soar and not be racked by doubts and guilt. I want to be wild and not give a damn.

Inch by inch he edged towards her.

His kiss was gentle. Caring.

Her heart fluttered in her chest.

She leant in for more. But he pulled away.

She wanted to scream. She wanted heat. More of him.

He was smiling when he pulled back.

But frowned as his gaze followed the big, fat tear that rolled down her cheek.

CHAPTER EIGHT

THEY STEPPED OUT onto the cathedral steps to thunderous applause. Kara blinked in the bright daylight, a gust of wind whipping her veil over her face. She scrambled to push it back, heard a chuckle, and then Edwin's strong, capable hands were helping, pushing the fine lace away, his gaze holding hers fondly, his fingertips settling wisps of her hair that had broken free.

Brace yourself, Kara. You can't cry again. Remember this is only all pretend. Don't get caught up in it. Know what is real and what isn't, for the sake of your sanity when this is all over and you have to walk away.

A chorus of 'Kiss! Kiss! Kiss!' rolled through the crowd. Edwin gave a teasing smile and the crowd reacted with good-natured laughter and then even more insistent calls for them to kiss.

Edwin turned to her, those golden eyes burning a path to her soul. An utterly convincing newlywed husband.

He's way too good at this pretence. But then, he was raised to present the image of utterly charming prince to the world. This is all second nature to him. Remember none of this is real.

His mouth touched hers. Her eyes closed, a deep shiver running down her spine.

The crowd erupted, their cheers echoing the boom in her heart.

Dammit. His kisses were perfection.

He pulled away, took her hand in his and led her to their awaiting carriage.

When they pulled away, Edwin took her hand in his and whispered against her ear, 'You look amazing and you're doing a fantastic job. The hard bit is over—try to relax and enjoy the rest of the day.'

How was she supposed to relax with the eyes of the world on her…and when he made her head spin with those kisses? 'You sound as if you're carrying out a work appraisal.'

He raised an eyebrow. 'I must make sure to give you a good bonus at the end of all this.'

Despite everything she felt herself blush, his flirting tone catching her by surprise.

All along their procession back to the palace they were greeted with shouts of goodwill and blessings for their marriage.

At the palace they and their families posed for formal photographs in the Oriental Room,

Edwin's steadying hand on the small of her back all the time.

And when they joined their guests for the pre-reception drinks he stayed at her side throughout, and she so wanted to allow herself to drift into a tantalising fantasy world where all of this was real.

A fantasy world that became even more entrancing when, during the intervals between the various wedding banquet courses, acts that Edwin had especially organised for her entertainment appeared on the ballroom stage.

A world-famous contemporary dancer perfectly enacted the words of one of Kara's favourite songs. And before the main course was served a legendary 1970s singer took to the stage. Kara, deep in shock, stared open-mouthed as the backing music to her most famous disco track began to play. Within seconds the entire room were out of their seats, dancing.

After the singer had finally left the stage, having performed three encores, Edwin hugged her, his thumb gently wiping the tears of happiness Kara couldn't hold back.

And then, before the dessert, Edwin stood to make his speech. He formally thanked the guests for their attendance and spoke for a few minutes on his plans for Monrosa, paying special attention to praising the impressive legacy he was inheriting from his father, who gave a brief satisfied nod in acknowledgement.

Then, folding the sheet of paper he was reading from, he waved it briefly in the air before saying, 'I've decided to deviate from the rest of my speech.' Turning, he addressed Kara directly. 'Today, in the cathedral, while I was waiting for your arrival, I began to panic. I thought that you might have changed your mind and wouldn't come.'

She shook her head—that had never been a consideration. Her arrival had been delayed thanks to a dog startling one of the horses along the route.

Edwin shrugged. 'I guess sometimes we need to face the worst possible scenario to fully appreciate what it is we have. You're my best friend. Kara, your loyalty, your intelligence, your humour all ground me. I know we're going to have an incredible partnership.' He paused and those golden eyes melted her heart. 'Thank you for being my wife.'

Then, turning to their guests, he raised his glass and said, 'Please join me in toasting my incredible wife, Kara, Princess of Monrosa.'

She smiled and smiled and acknowledged with a nod all those who rose and toasted her, her cheeks hurting, confusion, disappointment she had no right to feel making her heart thud in her chest.

Friendship…partnership…all the right words to describe their relationship. Had anyone noticed the absence of any mention of love in all of that? Or was it just her?

Changed into a blue trouser suit and white plimsolls, Triona at her side, Kara did a double-take of the now deserted ballroom.

Walking out onto the dance floor where earlier they had danced together, that disturbing chemistry rising between them and causing his heart to thud wildly, Kara said to Edwin, 'Please tell me you didn't end the party early? My dad's side of the family will never forgive you. They don't think it's a proper wedding if they don't get to see sunrise.'

Not waiting to draw breath, she planted her hands on her hips, her jacket parting to reveal an ivory silk camisole tucked into her trousers, her gaze shooting between him and Triona. 'What's going on? Why did I need to change out of my wedding dress?' She lifted her feet. 'And why the plimsolls?'

Triona gave him a look that said this was all on him, muttering she needed some air, and slipped out to the terrace, closing the door behind her.

Kara's suspicious gaze took in the open-necked dark blue shirt and lightweight navy trousers he had changed into.

He needed to make this marriage work. And the only way he knew how to do that was by trying to recapture what they had before he'd ever suggested marriage—a light, fun friendship with laughter and adventure and no complications or expectations.

He followed in Triona's footsteps, coming to a stop by the terrace door. 'I have a surprise for you.'

Her hands dropped from her hips. She edged up onto her toes to try to get a better glimpse out onto the terrace.

He opened the door and stepped outside, gesturing for her to follow.

She squinted out into the darkness and then eyed him with a frown.

But her curiosity obviously got the better of her because she walked towards him with an expression that said this surprise had better be good.

The moment she stepped outside a cheer went up from the awaiting guests who were lining both sides of the walkway down to the waterfront. And, as planned, the guests activated their light sticks in sequence, so that two rows of blue lights flowed all the way from the terrace down to the sea.

Kara screamed, gasped, and finally, thankfully, laughed.

She allowed him to guide her down the cobbled walkway, the guests swaying in time to the band's rendition of Kara's favourite song, 'Sunset Love'.

Kara's hand tightened around his as they made their way down the path of goodwill and celebration of their union. He smiled at Kara's laughter, relieved that so far he had made the right call in planning this goodbye to their guests.

The walkway led them to the palace's private marina and their awaiting families.

Kara dropped her hand from his and stared at *Mistral*, the royal yacht, and its crew, all lined up dockside in order to welcome them aboard. 'Please tell me they're not waiting for us.'

'I did promise you a honeymoon.'

'You said you were too busy.'

'I changed my mind.'

She glanced at all those around them, gave a faint smile towards the crew, and, edging closer to him, whispered, 'You know I get seasick.'

He laughed and gestured to the thirty-three metre boat with its five staterooms. 'I defy even you to get sick aboard *Mistral*. A superyacht is a very different experience to being on a racing yacht. Trust me, you'll be fine, and it's only three days' sailing on the Med.'

She blanched. 'Three days!' She stepped closer to the marina's edge, frowning at the waves. 'Those waves look big…why the hell couldn't we just have gone to some nice hotel or beach? Not that we needed to go away in the first place.'

The sea was choppier than he would have liked, but there was no way he was going to worry her by admitting that. 'You won't feel much movement on board *Mistral*.'

For that he received a disbelieving scowl.

He stepped closer to her. 'I know just how stressful the past few weeks have been for you. You deserve time away, a break.' He held her gaze, his heart swelling with his affection for her, his throat catching. 'It's time we hung out together like we used to, away from the glare of the palace staff and the media.' His throat tightened even more. 'It's time we recaptured our friendship.'

She let out a shaky breath. 'You're right… things have got so confusing.' She swung away to berate Triona, Siza and her parents for keeping the honeymoon secret from her.

Luis was attempting to charm one of Kara's cousins, who rightly was having none of it, so he went over to where his father and Ivo were standing together, not a word passing between them.

His joining them didn't help matters and all three eyed each other warily.

'Best of luck in…' He grimaced, trying to remember where Ivo's next major competitive regatta was to be held. He should have made more time to talk with him.

Ivo studied him and then his father, as though waiting to see if his father knew where his next regatta was.

His father simply shrugged.

'Plovdiv,' Ivo finally answered in a hacked-off tone before he walked away from them.

Edwin eyed his father, who held his gaze un-apologetically, a faint tic working in his jaw the only sign of any emotion. He turned away. This whole mess was his fault. He had turned his and Kara's lives upside down.

He went and waited for Kara to join him by the gangway.

She hugged her parents a brief goodbye, but with Triona and Siza she giggled and hung on to them for the longest time.

Why could he never be like that with people? What must it be like to be your true self? Not to feel apart and different?

As heir to the throne, he was always destined

to be different. People looked at him differently. Behaved differently around him. People were more of everything around him—more nervous, more gushing, more reserved, more self-conscious. And he had known, for as long as he could remember, that he had to behave appropriately—an inner critic constantly telling him to be careful and proper. An inner critic that over the years had escalated to tight inner control in the aftermath of his mother's death, where he was able to shut himself off from feeling too much for other people.

Kara turned away from her friends.

Rolled her shoulders as though bracing herself.

He rocked back on his heels. A realisation side-sweeping him. With him, Kara *did* hold herself back. It was as though an invisible wall existed between them. Even when they kissed there was a slight reservation, a hesitancy that was right and normal and proper. But it was also the most vulnerable place in the world.

Mistral eased away from the marina wall. Their guests cheered and waved, their blue lights dancing in the air like fireflies.

An explosion filled the air.

Kara jolted and grabbed hold of Edwin.

Gold and purple light filled the air.

Edwin chuckled.

She slapped him on the arm. 'You could have warned me.'

He raised an amused eyebrow. 'Come on, we'll see the display better on the opposite side.' He led her across the upper deck of the yacht, explosions of colours dancing overhead, the gold and purple of Monrosa giving way to the blue and red of the Union flag, and for a while she forgot just how cross she was with Edwin.

But that all changed once they left the natural protection of the harbour and hit the swell.

The boat pitched.

She grabbed the rail. Oh, God, it was only going to get worse once they were really out in open sea.

'I can't believe you thought a sailing holiday would be my idea of fun.' The boat pitched again as they rounded a headland, the swell growing higher. Exhausted from trying not to let the emotion of the day get to her, terrified she was going to spend the night throwing up, she added, 'I thought you knew me better.'

Edwin considered her for a moment, clearly trying to understand where her anger had come from.

Well, good. He could have at least talked this through with her.

'You're scared. That's understandable.' His

mouth tightened. 'But will you please just trust me on this?' With that he walked back across the deck and peered towards the building and street lights of the island, which were increasingly growing dimmer and dimmer.

Her anger deflated like a popped balloon. She felt herself redden. Now she just felt stupid.

Swallowing down her pride, she knew she had to do the right thing and show some gratitude. She went and stood next to him. 'How long have you been planning all of this?' she asked, pushing back the material of her suit jacket's lapel that had blown forward in the breeze. The suit was beautifully handcrafted, the silk lining soft against her skin. 'Who selected this suit? The shoes? Was it Princess Maria?'

His gaze trained out to sea, he answered, 'I did—it's that same shade as your eyes. The shoes were the most practical solution for our journey.' His tone was distracted.

He chose the suit? *Really?* A shiver ran down her spine. Here she was worrying about being seasick when in truth she really should be worried about the prospect of spending time alone with her new husband. He seemed to want it to be about them reconnecting as friends, which she was all up for. But what if they did something stupid like kiss again? Going away together, especially after last night, was like dancing with the devil. And it didn't help when he went and did something so cute and adorable and kind as select an outfit for her. One that he obviously had put thought and consideration into. Was he doing all of this just to keep her on-side? She winced at that thought, hating how cynical and wary she had become since Nick. God, she really did have trust issues. Staying well away from relationships really was the best thing for her.

She studied Edwin. What was he scanning the horizon for?

The engine of the yacht cut out. A whirring sound was followed by a splash. Was that the anchor being dropped?

Pointing in the direction of the silhouetted high cliff edges of Monrosa, Edwin said, 'This is where we disembark.'

Disembark? Already? They were miles away from land.

Squinting, she stared in the direction he had pointed in and realised a tiny dot of light was getting ever closer.

She followed Edwin down to the lower deck and then down to the platform at the rear of the boat.

That dot of light turned out to be Domenico and Lucas on board a small boat.

Pulling alongside, Lucas threw a rope to an

awaiting crew member, who held the boat tight against the yacht's platform. Domenico held his hand out, gesturing for her to transfer across.

Memories of the blood-curdling heat that had assaulted her insides the time she had been sea-sick had her hesitate.

A wave hit, pulling the boat away from *Mistral*, a huge gap of black sea opening up just beyond her feet. She stepped back. She was going nowhere.

The crew member and Lucas brought the boat back alongside.

Edwin leapt over onto the boat and held his hand out to her.

'There's no way you're getting me on that inflatable.'

He gave her a bemused look. 'Rib—not an inflatable. And a rib that's used for military patrols worldwide, so it's more than up to the job of transferring us back to Monrosa. When have *you* ever walked with lead feet?'

They were going back to Monrosa? That was a good thing, wasn't it? Was all of this just a hoax? Had he pretended they were going on a honeymoon to avoid speculation as to why they hadn't? Was he playing mind-games with her? Dread knotted in her stomach. Nick had once pretended to be taking her on a trip to Paris, only to cancel it after they had had an argument. She had only learnt he had never even booked their flights when she had broken up with him.

Edwin reached his hand out even further. 'Come on, I'll take care of you. Trust me.'

She studied his hand, both boats rocking in the swell. She trusted him. Of course she did.

'Kara?'

His voice was baffled. He was her friend. She had to trust him. Her feet refused to budge. But he wasn't just her friend any more...he was her husband. And trusting him now took on a whole different perspective. Could she trust him while still protecting her heart, her sanity, her grip on reality?

Enough.

She had to focus on the end game—raising the profile of Young Adults Together and helping Edwin to the throne.

She was allowing herself to get caught up in the emotion and drama of the day again, caught up in the concept of going on honeymoon with her new husband—which didn't look as though it was going to happen anyway, so why was she being such a drama queen?

She grabbed hold of Edwin's hand and leapt, colliding with him, her chest bumping against his. He steadied her, one warm and solid hand on her waist, the other on her back. The heat of his body fused with her limbs. His hold on her tightened. Without thinking she responded by edging her hips against his. The heat of longing fired in her stomach.

He dipped his head, his eyes narrowing as he slowly and silently studied her.

Undone by his nearness, feeling vulnerable under his gaze, she pulled away and attempted to act as though he had no effect on her pulse, which was racing so hard she was struggling to think straight. It felt as though every cell in her body was turned on by him. 'Where should I sit?'

He pointed to a seat at the centre of the boat alongside the cockpit.

Edwin took control of the wheel. She had thought Lucas would resume that duty. He pulled away from *Mistral* at an incredibly slow speed. At this rate they wouldn't reach Monrosa until daybreak.

'You do know what you're doing, right?'

He grinned. 'It was part of my training.'

Got him! 'Your special-forces training, you mean.'

His grin widened and he eased the throttle forward, pulling the rib into a wide arc.

The boat soared over the water. The wind rushed against her, making it difficult to breathe. She gasped. And laughed. The rush of water beneath them, the speed, watching Edwin expertly handle the rib, was exhilarating.

In no time they were slowing as they approached a slipway in an isolated cove.

Two SUVs were waiting for them.

Domenico and Lucas went in one, she and Edwin in the other.

The unpaved road out of the cove was steep and narrow; only a SUV would be capable of accessing the slipway.

At the main road, instead of turning left back towards Monrosa City Edwin turned right. Domenico and Lucas followed behind them.

'Aren't we going back to the palace?'

Edwin threw her a confused look. 'I told you we were going on a honeymoon.'

'Oh, I thought…'

'That I was going back on my word?' He worked his jaw, clearly annoyed. Tense seconds passed, and he shot a look towards her, his expression a horrible mix of disappointment and irritation. But then, with a shrug of his shoulder, he smiled. 'Sorry, but you're stuck with me for three whole days. I'll try to make it as painless as possible for you.'

Forty minutes later, having followed a hairpin-bend-laden road up into the mountains, they passed through the gates of Edwin's family's mountain villa, the sentries on duty saluting.

So this was where they would honeymoon.

She laid her head against the headrest and gave an internal sigh. She was a mountain girl. Walking amongst the towering pines and eucalyptus trees, the only sound coming from the breeze swooping through the valleys, trickling streams, and hidden birds happy to share their voices with the world, restored her. Being surrounded by this landscape that had existed for millennia before her always pulled her up to a sharp stop, grounding her in the reminder of just how transient life was and to be grateful for every day she got to enjoy it. But this would be different. They would be staying in a royal residence with all of its reminders of protocol. What she wouldn't give not to have to be on her best behaviour, to not have to act as if they were a loved-up couple on their honeymoon.

On a turn in the road, the vast royal residence in the distance, Edwin shot off the lit road and onto a narrow lane she had never spotted before.

Studying the side mirror, she said, 'You need to stop—we've lost Domenico and Lucas.'

'That was the plan. We're going to be on our own for the next three days.'

On their own? That was what she had just been longing for. Why, then, did it fill her with terror rather than relief? 'Please tell me we aren't going camping.'

He shook his head. 'Why are you being so cranky?'

She gave an indignant huff. But then did a mental eye roll. He was right. She was being cranky...and crabby and grouchy. She hated this side of herself. But being around Edwin nowadays she just felt this defensive force field around herself and it just seemed natural to be surly.

She needed to snap out of it. She held up her hand, her fingers in the Girl Guide pledge position she had learnt years ago. 'I promise to try harder and not moan even when I wake from dreaming of drinking cocktails on some tropical beach, only to find myself in a bug-infested tent.'

He grinned. 'That's more like it—it's good to see the old Kara back: good-humoured with an undertone of sarcasm.'

She snorted.

Edwin's eyes twinkled, and his grin grew even wider. She grinned back, heat infusing her limbs.

They climbed even further up into the mountain. Kara opened her window, the trees of the forest zipping by, and a perturbing mix of fear and exhilaration filled her bones at not only their crazy speed but also at the prospect of being alone with Edwin for three whole days.

The road ended at a set of wooden gates.

Edwin zapped them open.

Beyond the gates the road dipped down in a curve that brought them to a circular driveway.

Edwin killed the engine.

A light shone over a solitary wooden door of a flat-roofed, metal-panelled structure.

'We're staying in a shed?'

He opened his door. 'Well, that promise didn't last long.'

She climbed out of the car and joined Edwin on the gravelled driveway. He pressed a button on his phone. The door popped open.

Inside, the shed was in darkness. Edwin gestured for her to step inside. She folded her arms and refused to budge. 'This isn't where you turn out to be a psycho husband who holds me captive against my will in a shed in an isolated forest, is it?'

He raised an eyebrow, his smile suddenly as sexy as hell. 'It can be arranged if that's a fantasy of yours.' A look of pure masculine heat she had never seen before entered his eyes, setting alight a wild longing in her belly. 'I'm sure there are some ropes in the shed.'

Something very carnal and dangerous melted inside her. She sprang towards the door and leapt inside.

A row of internal lights, domino-style, lit up down the length of the building.

She gasped.

This was no shed.

She walked further into the long and narrow interior, agog at the gorgeous ultra-modern open-plan space. The walls, with the exception of the narrow entrance, were made of huge floor-to-ceiling glass doors. The modern kitchen was made from pale wood, the counter tops the same poured light-grey concrete as the floors. In the living area, two sofas covered in duckling-yellow fabric surrounded a wood-burning stove.

Edwin opened up a row of doors that folded back to reveal decking made from the same wood as the kitchen.

Walking out onto the deck, running the entire length of the building, she said, 'I can't believe that I thought this was a shed! It's absolutely stunning.'

The building was stretched like a bridge between two rocky banks, a stream running beneath the house.

Before them, the forest tumbled down the mountainside. Kara inhaled deeply, greedily sucking in the heavily pine-scented air.

'Do you like it?'

She turned at Edwin's question. She gestured

around her and laughed. 'This is my idea of heaven. Of course I love it.'

'Good. It's my wedding present to you.'

Kara watched him turn away and walk inside, her mouth open.

She rushed after him as he walked towards the far end of the house, which they had not yet explored.

She caught up with him at a bedroom door. 'But all I got you was a set of cufflinks.'

He leant against the door frame. 'You're forgetting the *How To Be a Good Husband* guide that came with them.'

'I hope you took note of point five—"Let her know you realise how lucky you are to have her as your wife".'

'Duly noted. My legal team have the paperwork ready for you to sign to give you full ownership of Villa Kara.'

She swung her arms up into the air in horror. 'Villa Kara! Are you serious? You have to change that name and I can't accept a villa from you. This was never mentioned in the pre-nup. You know I don't want anything when we divorce.'

'You just said you love it here—as I had hoped you would.' He folded his arms. 'Are you saying you're refusing my wedding present to you?'

How did he manage to make it sound as though she was being thoroughly unreasonable and ungrateful? When it was he who was at fault here? 'It's way too generous, and what happens when we split up? I can hardly drive through your family's property to get here.'

'Why not?'

'Because it'll be as awkward as hell.'

His amused expression disappeared. He straightened from his relaxed leaning against the door frame. 'When we divorce…if we divorce—that's still your decision to make—you'll still be an important part of my life.'

She sagged against the opposite wall, suddenly feeling exhausted. She dipped her head, uncertainty and fear sweeping through her, causing her heart to contract as though it was under attack. She should let this go. She knew she should. Just continue pretending they'd resume life as before, pretending their friendship was not already damaged by this whole experience. 'Do you really think we will be able to part so amicably—without any hurt or complications?'

Those golden eyes considered her for long silent seconds. She resisted the urge to cry, to laugh. How had she ended up in the position where she was being torn between the desire to kiss this man and to punch him for not feeling the same confusion and turmoil as she did? Had their kisses had any emotional impact on him?

'It's up to us to make sure we part amicably.' With that he turned and walked into the bedroom.

Like the living area it had floor-to-ceiling windows overlooking the forest. Edwin went and opened one of the two doors either side of the king-size bed, draped in crisp white cotton linen and accented with a green throw and cushions. 'This is your dressing room—your bathroom is on the other side. Your luggage was brought here earlier.'

It was disconcerting to see the faded black jeans she had bought in a shop in Brighton hanging from the rail, a solid crease line running the length of both legs showing that someone had carefully ironed them.

Her gaze moved to the bed. And then back to Edwin.

He cleared his throat. 'My bedroom is across the corridor.'

So they wouldn't be sleeping in the same bed on their wedding night after all. It made sense and would eliminate any awkwardness. Why, then, did it feel like a rejection?

She breathed in deeply. Stepped back to make space for him to leave. Smiled. 'It's been a long day—I need a shower and sleep. A lot of sleep. I'm exhausted. Worn out.'

She stopped. He had probably got the point the first time.

He nodded and moved towards the door.

She breathed in hard when he passed her. Was about to exhale, but he came to a stop a footstep beyond her. He turned. 'Please tell me you'll accept Villa Kara? It's important to me.'

Her entire body tingled from having him stand so close by, by the appeal of his gaze that was utterly focused and determined. 'Why?'

'Because it will mean that you'll still want to be in my life.'

She closed her eyes, uncertainty, confusion, sheer bewilderment over the beautiful intention of his words clashing with her fears for the future of their relationship.

She opened her eyes. 'The first thing I'm going to do is change its name—Villa Kara is one hundred per cent cringe.'

CHAPTER NINE

SITTING ON THE stone ledge, her feet dangling in the stream, Kara tossed her head back to catch the rays of sunlight breaking through the overhead tree canopy. Her denim cut-offs suited her perfectly and her white halter-neck…well, as much as he hated to admit it, it was troublingly sexy. It was just a piece of simple white cotton after all, but the way it pulled on her chest, its cut exposing all but a few inches of her shoulders, got to him in a way it shouldn't.

The sun caught the platinum shades in her hair, the ends brushing against the dusty surface of the ledge.

How was he going to cope with sharing a bed with her when back in the city? When they returned to the reality of their lives away from this oasis of escape?

They had spent three days trekking in the mountains by day, cooking meals together and playing poker at night, Kara cheekily refusing to admit she tried to cheat every single time. Three days of conversation and teasing. Three days of pretending she wasn't getting under his skin. Yesterday he had become obsessed at the idea of undoing the pearl buttons of the blue embroidered blouse she had been wearing and had even burnt himself when distracted as they had been preparing dinner, scorching the tip of his finger on a hot pan. Three days of resisting the urge to kiss her, of averting his gaze from her bottom when she trekked ahead of him. Three days of resisting the urge to hunker down to retie her laces, which she never knotted properly, knowing that if he knelt before her his fingers would trail against the now lightly tanned skin of her legs, trace over the small brown birthmark at the back of her right knee. Three days of his heart dancing to hear her laughter, to see her blue eyes widen in amazement when a red kite swooped close to where they had been picnicking, her hand reaching for his. Three days of quickly ending their celebratory hugs when they reached the summit of their climbs.

And two nights of her closing her bedroom door to him.

Two nights of sitting out on the terrace staring at the stars, unable to sleep, listening to a nightjar filling the air with its constant song.

Two nights of journeying through that labyrinth of hopes and fears and thoughts in the middle of the night, of wondering if the chemistry, those fleeting looks that electrified him, were all in his imagination or if she bore their curse too.

Dio! To think that a week ago he had actually considered cancelling his tour to Asia. Now it was his lifeline. In two days' time they would make their first appearance together as a married couple when they attended the opening of a new conservation centre in Monrosa's protected wetlands, named in honour of his mother. And the day after, he would leave for Asia. Ten days away would clear his head, give him the space to get back on track with this marriage of convenience.

They had one more night alone before they returned to the city. He *had* to continue keeping his distance from her.

He dropped the picnic blanket to the ground. Her eyes popped open and she smiled. 'Hi.'

He nodded back, unfurling a picnic blanket beside her, trying to steady his pulse. When she was so obviously delighted to see him it did crazy things to his heart.

Kara edged onto the blanket and he sat beside her, dipping his own bare feet into the stream. Maybe the icy water would cool the heat in his body.

Lifting her feet from the water, she wriggled her toes. 'You'll be glad to hear my feet are no longer aching.'

Her toes were long, her feet narrow with a delicate arch. She lifted her feet even higher, circling them. Her ankles were slim, her calf muscles toned.

What would it be like to have her legs wrapped around his?

He grabbed the champagne bottle from the basket, popped it open. He passed her a glass.

She sighed. 'This is heaven.'

For the next half an hour they drank the champagne and nibbled on the fresh bread they had baked together that morning, using an olive-oil-based recipe Kara swore by. The sun was gentle, the birdsong and sound of the water pressing over the boulders in the stream hypnotic. A lazy sense of calm had his body grow increasingly heavy, his thoughts drowsy.

Champagne finished, Kara lay back on the blanket with a sigh and he joined her, the hard stone beneath him a welcome solidness. They lay with their feet side by side, drying them on the edge of the rock ledge.

Kara swayed her bent knees side to side, her hands on her belly, her gaze in his direction, a wide smile on her mouth. 'I think the champagne has gone to my head.'

'Mine too,' he admitted. 'I guess the long trek and lack of lunch probably didn't help.'

Above them a buzzard soared in the thermals.

His heart rate upped a gear. Without looking he knew Kara was staring at him. He closed his eyes. He was *not* going to look in her direction. He should make some excuse and leave.

'I'm very jealous of your long eyelashes, you know.'

He opened his eyes and turned to her. Her eyes held a soft, dewy tone. Her lips glistened as though the champagne had seeped into them. Gentle heat infused her cheeks.

Her hand shifted off her belly and onto the blanket between them. 'I'll miss you when you're away.'

He sucked in some air. *Dio!* He really should head back to the villa. 'And I'll miss you.'

Why had he said that? Because it was true.

Qualify it... Don't go down a road that will be hard to come back from.

'Touring can be boring—it would be nice to have you there for company.'

She looked away from him but not before he saw the disappointment that dispatched her smile.

She bit her lip for a moment before saying, 'And I have the Pink Heart's charity ball to attend. It will be my first official duty on my own.' She looked back at him, gave a shrug. 'I'll miss having your guidance.'

'I've asked Princess Maria to travel with you to the ball and sit at the same table.'

She gave a fleeting smile. 'Thank you.'

His hand found hers on the blanket.

Her eyes widened. He held his breath, waiting for her reaction. Her fingers threaded through his.

A question appeared in her gaze.

'I guess it's understandable that things might get a little muddled between us at the start of the marriage,' he said.

'Muddled?'

'The emotion of the wedding, being alone, neither of us having been in a relationship for a long time...our hormones, our feelings, are getting muddled up.'

She nodded eagerly. 'And the champagne isn't helping either.'

Why is this...this...? Dio! *Call it what it is. Why is this flirting so damn enjoyable?*

He cleared his throat, his eyes glued to her mouth, memories of what it was like to kiss her heading straight to his groin. 'I want to kiss you.'

She shifted onto her side. 'Good.'

He released her hand. Moved onto his side too, edged up to her. Ran his hand through her hair. It was warm. As was her cotton top. Even the denim of her shorts held the heat of the day. He placed his hand on her bottom. Pulled her even closer. Found her mouth with a groan.

They kept it soft and exploratory for the whole of ten seconds.

Then her hand clasped against his skull, her mouth opening for him.

He rolled onto his back, taking her with him. And saw stars when her body rocked against his. He held tight, his arms on her back, one hand cupping her bottom, the other a sharp shoulder blade, wanting to meld her to him.

Within a minute things were seriously getting out of control. Kara was moaning against his mouth, her legs twisted around his. Her chest pressed against his was the sweetest, most dangerous, most tempting thing that had ever entered his life.

His thumb stroked the side of her breast. Her body shuddered.

Her mouth shifted away from his and began to trail down his throat, her lips scorching the skin beneath his open-neck T-shirt.

Her hands trailed even further south.

Pleasure blasted through him. With a groan he pulled her back up towards him, cradling her face in his hands. 'We can't.'

Her expression shifted from unseeing desire

to frustration to disappointment and finally acceptance on a long inhale of breath.

She rolled off him.

He held her hand. 'Are you okay?'

'In a few minutes I will be.' She rolled her eyes. 'These blasted hormones—they have a lot to answer for.'

He sat up, allowed his blood pressure to settle and stood up.

He yanked off his T-shirt and then his shorts.

Kara gawked at him, a hand covering her mouth.

He spun around and jumped into the deep pool of water beyond a large boulder, a spray soaring upwards as he plunged beneath the cold water.

Even submerged, he heard Kara's shriek.

CHAPTER TEN

THE CENTRAL COURTYARD of the Senator Hotel had been transformed into a Viennese ballroom. Chandeliers hung from invisible wires, and a full orchestra played on the temporary stage. Dancing with Javier Ventosa, a paediatrician consultant at Monrosa's University Hospital, Kara tried to focus on her steps and turns, her head spinning at the quick rotations, only too aware Princess Maria was following her every move, just as she had done all week when she had supervised Kara's dance lessons.

Mastering the steps of the Viennese waltz had been excruciatingly slow, she had tripped over her dance teacher, Horacio, more times than she could count and she had used the feeble excuse that she was more of a rugby girl to explain to Princess Maria her lack of progress when in truth it was her nephew who had stolen her concentration away.

They had been so close to making love. And a

week on, her focus was still shot and a throb of unfulfilled lust was making her rubber-boned. A week on and she still couldn't strip him from her mind, that image of him yanking off his top and shorts and plunging into the stream, soaking her in the process, playing on a constant loop. He had emerged all wet, glistening muscle, frustration etched on his face.

In silence he had walked away from her and she had collapsed back onto the ledge, weak with the need for more.

Dinner that night had been tense. Their conversation had been halting and awkward and full of things unsaid.

When he had left for Vietnam, his hug goodbye had been brief and she had watched him get into the car taking him to the airport and had winced at the relief that had swept over his expression.

He had wanted to get away.

Mortified by his relief, she had thrown herself into work, into settling into her new life in Monrosa, taken dance lessons in advance of tonight, and spent her evenings walking the interior of the palace and grounds, trying to familiarise herself with her new home.

A few times she had considered travelling to Villa Kara, driven by the need to find some antidote to the constant confusion settling into her bones. Confusion driven by his infrequent calls to her, which were full of facts but absent of any real truth between them.

The mountains usually brought her peace and in the private isolation of Villa Kara she might have been able to eke out some calmness. But memories of their stay there had kept her away. Memories of how Edwin had looked every morning when she had opened her bedroom door to find him freshly showered and preparing breakfast in the kitchen, his good-morning smile managing to ignite a furnace of happiness inside of her. Memories of his deep laughter when she had got stuck when rock climbing, but then his calm words of encouragement in guiding her back down.

Trying to create a new life in a new country, the pressures of royal life, trying to map out precisely how she was going to turn Young Adults Together into an effective global charity, were all making her vulnerable...and if her past history was anything to go by, when she was stressed and confused she was prone to making bad decisions. Very bad decisions. Decisions like sleeping with Edwin even though it would torpedo any hopes of their maintaining their friendship when this was all over. Some people managed to remain friends with their exes but there was no way she could do it. She simply didn't have the emotional toughness for it. She would find it impossible not to feel exposed and heart-sore knowing what once had been there.

See, this was why she wasn't cut out for relationships—she just became an emotional mess when embroiled in them. She was better off in the safety of singledom. She needed time to adjust to her new reality. Time to let the emotional fever inflamed by what the media had called a fairy-tale wedding ceremony and the promises they had made in public, die away.

The music came to a stop.

Javier bowed his thanks to her for accepting his invitation to dance. He was an incredibly attractive man...and single too. But not one cell in her body seemed capable of responding to his dark looks and charming smile.

She accepted his hand and offer to escort her back to her table.

But then she dropped his hand, the hairs on the back of her neck standing to attention.

Javier stepped back and bowed to someone behind her.

And backed away.

A dovecote-full of fluttering exploded in her stomach.

'I never knew my wife could dance so well.'

Longing pure and unadulterated flushed through her body at his low whisper.

She swung around. She wanted to throw herself into his arms but caught herself in time.

Instead she smiled at him goofily, heat blasting her cheeks. 'You're home.'

All through her dance with Javier, whom he had first met when opening the new children's wing of MUH, Edwin had stayed in the shadows of the courtyard watching Kara as she glided across the floor in Javier's arms. Lust and jealousy had him barely clinging to his sanity. He had wanted to march onto the dance floor and interrupt the dance midway, demand the right to dance with his wife.

His wife. His beautiful wife. *Dio!* Her ballgown was the sexiest thing he had ever seen. It was a dress that summed up her personality—the pale blue, close to silver tulle skirt overlaid with floral appliqué, cute and lovely just as she was, the plunging front and back the hidden side of her that was all heat and passion.

'You're home.'

Had words ever seemed so sweet, so right, so layered with danger?

He searched for some light-hearted response, but the delight shining in Kara's eyes stole every word away.

He held out his hand and invited her to dance with him.

Around them, other couples who had already begun to circle the dance floor smiled fondly at their reunion.

She stepped into his arms. He longed to be able to pull her close, anchor her to him, but the waltz demanded an exasperating distance be kept between their bodies.

'Why are you home early?' she asked.

'There's still a lot of work that has to be done in preparation for my succession.'

And I missed you.

'How was Hanoi?'

'Hot and chaotic but very beautiful. I loved it there.'

He *had* loved Hanoi, but he had felt flat there. He had longed to have Kara by his side, experiencing the infectious chaos of the city and the stunning beauty of the surrounding countryside. He had missed her laughter, the appraising sweep of her blue gaze, the way his body tingled when she was in the same room. *Dio*, he was so sick of pretending his feelings for Kara had not changed, when they had. She was no longer just a friend. She was his wife. Lying in his hotel bedroom two nights ago, he had finally admitted to himself that he wanted her. As a husband wanted a wife. He wanted to sleep with her, mouth against mouth, breath against breath, skin against skin.

The pretending had to stop.

'I missed you,' he said.

Her gaze shot up to meet his. She frowned as though she was trying to decipher the true meaning of his words.

Her lips parted. Those glorious soft lips… Thoughts of what they were capable of had tormented his dreams for the past week.

The music came to an end. Instead of stepping back, Kara touched her fingers against the skin above his shirt collar, an intimate move that had relief and raw need buckling his knees. 'I missed you too.'

He gathered her closer. Placed a kiss on her neck, just below her ear.

They stayed on the dance floor until the orchestra played the final song of the night. They said their goodbyes to the event organisers and he led her out of the private exit, where Álvaro and Marco, their assigned protection officers, were waiting for them. Domenico and Lucas had made a poor attempt at disguising their delight when he had announced he was cutting his trip short. Their eagerness to get home to their families had sent his head into a spin. Why was he jealous of something he didn't want?

He had told them to take the next three days off work.

They drove in silence through the streets of

Monrosa. Tourists and locals, leaving the restaurants of the old town, stopped to stare as the outriders passed them by, grabbing their phones to snatch a photo as their SUV driven by Álvaro swept past.

He held Kara's hand, her fingers clasping his tight.

Back at their apartment, he instructed both Simone his valet and Cecilia, Kara's dresser, who were awaiting their return, that their services weren't needed.

He brought her into the drawing room, knowing he was at a fork in the road that was his life.

He gestured towards the drinks cabinet but Kara shook her head.

This would be their first night of needing to share a bed.

The decisions he would take, *they* would take, in the next few minutes could alter their lives for ever.

But they were both adults. Capable of handling uncharted territory.

He cleared his throat. Lost for words.

Kara touched her hand to her breastbone, giving him an uncertain and fleeting smile.

'Tonight…' he faltered.

She moved forward from where she had been balancing her fingertips against the side table

filled with gold and silver framed family photographs towards the marble fireplace. 'Yes?'

There was a new framed photograph on the
side table. He went and lifted the heavy silver
frame. It was a signed photograph from their
wedding photographer, Patrizia Mauro, of them
waving to the crowd as they had emerged from
the cathedral. Kara's eyes were sparkling. The
perfect image of a bride overcome with emotion. He cleared his throat again. 'Tonight…
we'll be sharing a bed.'

Kara inhaled deeply. 'Yes.'

He winced at the dread in her voice. 'I can
sleep on the floor…'

'No! Of course not.'

It really was time for the pretending to stop.
He bunched his hands.

But would the truth destroy everything?

'If we sleep in the same bed…'

He lowered the frame to the table, catching
a glimpse of his parents' wedding photograph.
They had had a good marriage despite its having been arranged. Could Kara and he come to
some sort of arrangement that would work for
them?

'I'm attracted to you and I've missed you. I
want to kiss you again. And I'd prefer for it not
to stop there.' Unsteadied by his admission, he

paused. Had he just made the biggest, most embarrassing blunder of his life?

He waited for Kara to say something, but instead she walked past him and out into the corridor.

He followed her, unsure what was happening.

In their bedroom, she stood at the near edge of the bed, her back to him. 'Cecilia was going to help me undress, so I'll need you to unbutton my gown for me.'

A lick of desire travelled the length of his body at the huskiness of her voice. He fumbled with the button holding the material tight to her waist, his fingers beating like nervous bats against her lower back. The button, once he got his fingers under control, gave way easily. He shifted his head down to her ear. 'I'm guessing you could have easily undone that yourself.'

She shivered, her neck tilting away from his breath. 'Yes, but there would have been no fun in that, would there?'

He touched a finger to her spine. She arched her back.

'I've spent the entire week away thinking about you.'

She twisted her head. Her eyes, even in the faint light cast by the single lamp in the corner, glittered. 'In a good way, I hope.'

'I'm afraid not.' He liked her groaned response. A lot. His fingertip bumped over the knots of her spine and then his whole hand fanned out to sweep across the edge of her shoulder blade, his skin tingling at the soft warmth of her body.

He edged the material of her dress off her shoulders. She drew her head back and whispered, 'Tell me what you've been thinking.'

He touched his lips to her collarbone. 'Our kiss, the pattern of your ribs,' he edged closer to her neck, he nipped her skin between his teeth, chuckled to hear her moan, 'your sighs of pleasure when I touch somewhere tender.'

She turned to him, her hands holding the material of her dress from falling down. Fire and energy radiated from her. 'Tell me what you want.'

'I want to make love to you.'

She nodded. Dropped her hands. Her dress fell to the floor.

She stood before him, naked except for pale blue panties.

He drew in a breath. She was more beautiful than he had ever imagined.

She arched her back and, reaching up, released her hair from its coil. It tumbled down over her shoulders.

He undid his bow tie. Pointed to the buttons of his dress shirt. 'Your turn.'

CHAPTER ELEVEN

CRUSHED SHEETS. Aching and deliciously heavy bones.

Kara grinned and twisted onto her side. Sleep called to her, but just out of reach gorgeous memories wound their way through her dazed brain.

She sighed.

'Your sighs of pleasure when I touch somewhere tender...'

Her eyes shot open. The room was in darkness. Water was running in the bathroom.

She curled the top sheet over her head and groaned.

What had she done?

Had she really done those things with Edwin? She flung the sheet back, struggling for air.

Everything was going to be okay.

This was still a marriage of convenience. Their relationship might have shifted off centre from friendship but the roller coaster of emotions, the power play, the constant threat of heartache that came with a full-blown relationship wouldn't apply to them.

The water was switched off. Shadows moved on the white marble floor of the bathroom.

She sat up in the bed, yanking the sheet up to her shoulders. Would she have time to dash into the dressing room? No! She couldn't bear the thought of him seeing her naked.

Why didn't you care last night, when it mattered? Because you were lost to the joy of seeing him again? Lost in the intimacy of his words, his touch? Lost to the chemistry that experiencing the powerful act of marrying had unleashed on you?

She had to play it cool. Not freak out. Not overthink all of this.

The bathroom door swung fully open.

Edwin stood there, a towel tight on his narrow hips, beads of moisture on his chest.

He gave her a devastating, satisfied smile that slowly morphed into a tender, almost bashful grin. He tilted his head, ran a towel over his hair and walked towards the bed. 'Good morning, my lovely wife.'

A storm of panic passed through her.

'We made a mistake.'

His smile evaporated.

'What?'

His hair was all tousled and sexy. But his expression was one hundred per cent perplexed.

She shivered despite the fact that her insides were scorching, churning chaos.

'We shouldn't have slept together.'

He flicked a hand over his hair, fixing it into position, his mouth tightening. 'Why?'

She didn't know why. She just knew she was drowning in panic. What was the matter with her? Why was she saying these things? Her panic rose like a tide that would never recede. 'You know why. It's just going to make our divorce more complicated.'

He flung the towel towards the bathroom. It hit the door frame and smacked onto the wooden floor of the bedroom. 'Are you saying you regret sleeping with me?'

She closed her eyes. 'No.'

'So what are you saying?'

Put some clothes on. I can't think straight, remembering how my hands, my lips, touched every inch of you. How I refused to stop even when you begged me to. I needed to know every inch of you. I wanted to know you... I've spent a decade wanting to know you. I've spent a decade wanting to love you.

Unable to breathe, she blinked.

I love you. Oh, God, I love you. This can't be happening. I'm messing everything up. And if you find out I'll just want to die. Will you feel

*sorry for me? Will you find excuses to walk
away? Or will you, like Nick, use it against me?*

She lifted the sheet even higher, gathering
the edges around her neck. 'Don't you think it
was a mistake?'

His mouth tightened even more. He turned
away, grabbed the towel from the floor, disappeared into the bathroom for a moment, returned and then went into his dressing room.

An agonising time later he emerged, flicked
on her bedside lamp and studied her. He had
changed into a dark grey suit, silver tie and
white shirt. Brooding and hacked off.

He knows! Her cheeks flamed. 'I'm sorry.'

His mouth tightened. And then with a sigh
he sat down on the bed beside her.

She wanted to leap out of the bed, escape
from him, but she was naked, and she and her
shredded dignity couldn't handle the thought of
him analysing every imperfection of her body
as she wobbled towards the bathroom.

He dipped his head, his hand moved as
though to touch her leg beneath the sheet but
he grabbed it back. They had made love endless
times during the night, drunk on physical re-
lease. Drunk on whispered words of discovery,
of tenderness between two people who knew
each other but whose souls, whose secret in-

ternal selves were a mystery they were just discovering.

He looked back up, his expression closed. 'Last night wasn't a mistake. We're attracted to one another.' He paused and shrugged as though that fact was of little significance. 'These things happen when two people are in close proximity. Let's keep it in perspective. It was one night.' He stood up, his expression emotionless. 'It doesn't have to happen again.'

She faked a smile, while her heart was on the floor. 'I guess we got it out of our systems.'

He shrugged again, and, taking his phone from his pocket, he checked the screen and frowned. 'I have a cabinet meeting I need to attend.'

Halfway towards the bedroom door, he turned around. 'Will you be okay?'

She heard the concern in his voice. She nodded. 'Of course.'

He left the room and she closed her eyes, curling onto her side, inhaling his scent on the sheets.

She was in love with him. She was in love with her husband.

She closed her eyes, hating the vulnerability of that. Hating that it weakened her, made her susceptible to so much pain and humiliation and disappointment.

She jerked the sheet back, sprang out of the bed and in the bathroom switched on the shower.

Her diary was full for the day. If Edwin could walk away from last night so easily, then she sure as hell was going to do the same thing. How many times had she seen her dad reach out to her mum, only to be rejected and humiliated? How many times had she tried to please Nick, only to encounter a snide comment or whatever mind game he had decided to indulge in that day?

She was not going to humiliate herself. She was going to behave with dignity and pride both within this marriage and when it was time for them to separate.

And just maybe, with the passage of time and aided by Edwin's interpretation of last night as having been of no particular consequence, she might be able to stuff her feelings for him so deep inside of her, even she would be able to disregard them.

Edwin's father glared at the organisation chart he had just distributed to the cabinet so intently Edwin wouldn't have been surprised if it spontaneously combusted.

'These changes aren't necessary. You're over-complicating things. Why on earth do we need a social-media team, a technology minister?' His voice growing ever louder, his father added, 'A diversity and equality minister? What on earth will *his* contribution be?'

'*Her* contribution, you mean. I have already selected a candidate for the role—Sofia Dati, Professor of Equality Studies at Monrosa University.'

Pausing, he studied the cabinet he was inheriting from his father, the majority of whom were men who had been in their roles for far too long.

'It's my intention to reshuffle this cabinet too. Reassign roles. Change the nature of each department's responsibilities to reflect the challenges we face as a country—our need to be more responsive and responsible to the environment, the changing diversity of our population and the need for a more advanced communication infrastructure that will attract even more companies to our business hubs.'

His patience thin, his ability to concentrate even thinner, he cut across his father before he could utter a word of objection, 'We've covered enough ground for today. I'm calling an end to this cabinet session.'

The ministers were regarding him with a variety of expressions from nervous to aghast and outraged. He couldn't afford to alienate them, not with their experience and influence within the country, which he would need in the coming months. He had to bring them with him on this journey of change, even if it meant dragging some of them kicking and screaming into the twenty-first century. 'I will meet with each of you individually to discuss aligning your experience and interests with the new structure. Change can be daunting, but we have to embrace it to ensure we are meeting the needs of our people. We have an exciting future ahead of us.'

At least a few of those around the table smiled at his words—albeit nervously.

He left the cabinet room, his footsteps the only sound. Even his father seemed to have been stunned into silence.

He walked in the direction of his offices. He had a call with the Swedish Trade Minister in an hour. Then a meeting with his own Finance Minister and his team, where discussions on budget reallocations would undoubtedly get heated. A meeting after that with the succession-ceremony logistics team.

He needed to remain focused and present. And not give in to the disbelief pounding through him.

He entered his outer offices, Victor's team all turning in his direction. Maribel, his travel coordinator, stood up, holding a pile of documentation in her grasp.

He couldn't do this. He couldn't discuss his trip next month to Washington.

He backed out of the room.

Out in the corridor he flung open the nearest door into the gardens.

He bolted down the terraces, ignoring the curious glances from the gardening team, until he came to the waterfront.

He sucked in air greedily but the tightness in his chest refused to give.

He cursed, the thin layer of denial that had got him through the cabinet meeting melting. To be replaced by the sharp kick of shame.

He had let himself down. He had let his country down. And, most importantly of all, he had let Kara down. She had agreed to their marriage in good faith. She hadn't signed up for him to seduce her.

No wonder she had immediately regretted it, considered it a mistake.

What had he expected? That she would have been happy with the fantasy he had imagined in the shower this morning of them sleeping in the same bed every night and fulfilling each other's needs?

He had walked out of the bathroom intending to wake Kara by kissing the length of her spine, and instead had faced her bruised eyes and horrified expression.

Maybe he should be grateful that at least one of them was thinking straight and saw it for the mistake that it was rather than feeling as though someone had punctured his ego and kicked it down the street like a rusty old can.

He had to make this right. Do the correct thing after a night of making the wrong decision over and over again.

He found her in her office, staring out of the window towards the internal courtyard.

Was she thinking of their engagement announcement out there? Their first kiss?

He called out her name.

She startled and whipped around. Wearing wide-legged pink trousers and a white blouse, her hair tied back in a ponytail, the crispness of her appearance was in sharp contrast to the tiredness in her eyes.

He worked his jaw, hating the unease between them.

'We can separate.'

Her head jerked back. 'Is that what you want?'

No, what I want is to kiss you, to bring you back to my bed and lose myself in you like I did last night. I want to go back in time to when our relationship was easy and straightforward. When I hadn't been pulled under into a world of chaos by the chemistry that our first kiss, out there in that courtyard, unleashed.

'What I want isn't of importance.'

Kara's expression tightened. 'I asked you a question Edwin, do you want to separate?'

'If it will make you happier.'

She folded her arms. 'It was a yes or no question.'

He cleared his throat, frustration bubbling up inside of him. Why was she making this so hard? He should lie, make all of this easier. But the least she deserved was his honesty. 'No I don't want us to separate but after last night—'

'Why?'

He swallowed and blurted out, 'Because I want to somehow make this right, and if we separate now it probably won't ever be right between us again.'

She winced and on a long sigh she considered him. Her eyes were so terribly sad.

He had really got this all so wrong.

'What do you mean by "make this right"?'

'I want things to go back to where they were, when we were friends.'

Seconds passed. She studied him with a perplexed expression. She went and stared down to an open diary on her desk. 'I have a teleconference call in ten minutes with a Greek mental health charity who are interested in rolling out the Young Adults Together model as part of their work.' Her gaze swept up to meet his, her expression cool. 'I'd like to think we are both mature enough to put the importance of our work before any regrets.'

CHAPTER TWELVE

THE SCRAPE OF a door handle turning. Silence. Eyes closed, she waited for the mattress to compress. But there was only a stillness. She opened her eyes. The bed beside her was empty. She darted a look at the door, listened for a sound from the bathroom. Nothing. Had she imagined the door opening?

Her hand moved out, patting the cool sheets, the vast emptiness.

Where was he?

Disorientated but knowing it was some time in the early hours of the morning, she grappled to turn on the bedside lamp. Then fumbled for her phone in the bedside locker drawer.

Her hands shook. He had *never* not come to bed in the two weeks since they'd slept together.

She typed out a message.

Where are you?

Waiting, desperate for the phone to ping, she imagined him in an accident. Had he gone out on his motorbike? What if he was with another woman? No. He wouldn't do that.

Her phone pinged. She jolted, the chime an invasion of the silence of the room.

I'm in my office.

She hurled the phone across the bed. The bed where they had explored each other's bodies. She sprang off the mattress and, pulling on her dressing gown, she bolted out of the bedroom and across the corridor.

Her dress, on a silk padded clothes hanger, hung from the dark wood freestanding mirror of her old bedroom, which nowadays functioned as her hair and make-up room. Later this morning a team would once again magically transform her from Kara Duffy to Her Serene Highness, Princess of Monrosa.

Transform her on the outside. Inside she knew she was a fraud. Pretending to be a princess. Acting out, in an ever so careful and measured way her love and devotion for her new husband, desperately hiding the truth of her real, visceral love for him. Especially from him.

And today was what it was all about. His enthronement. The first day he would reign as Monarch of Monrosa.

She eyed her dress for the ceremony again. It was a dress that simply was. It made no demands. No statement. Below-the-knee length with cap sleeves, the ivory cotton tweed shot with threads of gold, it was elegant and understated. It conformed. It was a grown-up's dress in the serious world of power and politics and duty and service.

It represented everything she had to become.

She touched the soft tweed, tiredness washing over her. She should go back to bed. Today was going to be exhausting with both the enthronement and the celebration ball afterwards to attend. An entire day of public scrutiny where she had to act the dutiful and proud wife and hide her constant heartache, her real, authentic, frantic, soul-destroying love for her husband.

She turned, her steps immediately faltering.

Edwin was standing at the door.

She pulled the lace edges of her dressing gown together, feeling exposed in her nightwear while Edwin was dressed in black trousers and a lightweight black cashmere jumper. Gorgeous in a tired and crumpled way.

For a nanosecond she felt tenderness for him. She wanted to hold his hand and lead him to their bed. Hold him while he slept.

But then a wave of anger, of fear, of raw vulnerability swept through her. 'If you decide not to come home, at least have the courtesy to tell me.'

He blinked at her fury. 'We need to talk.'

He wasn't only exhausted, he was also nervous. Was he about to end their marriage? Their friendship? Was he too worn out by the pretence of their marriage?

She lifted her chin. Determined to be dignified. She would *never* let him even glimpse her devastation.

He held up the ivory sheet of paper in his hand, the crown's gold insignia on the top. 'My enthronement pledge. I'd like to read it to you.'

Where was this conversation going? She wanted to say no. She was in no mood to talk about his enthronement but, seeing how his hand trembled as he held out the heavy page towards her, appealing for her to say yes, she nodded.

'I do here solemnly swear to govern the people of Monrosa in accordance with the laws and customs of our country. I promise to rule with fairness and integrity, serving to the best of my ability, always with the utmost honesty.'

With a sigh he lowered the paper. 'With the utmost honesty.' He grimaced and inhaled another breath as though starved of oxygen. 'How can I promise to serve with honesty when I'm not honest with either you or myself?'

His voice was husky, as though it was taking a huge effort even for him to speak.

She swallowed hard, her fingernails biting into her closed fists. It was all over, then.

She moved towards the door, her gaze focused on the dark corridor behind him. The media would camp outside her Brighton apartment. 'I need to call my dad.'

His hand reached out as she neared him. 'It's five in the morning.'

She pulled her arm away so that he couldn't touch her. 'I can slip out of Monrosa before everyone wakes. We can go to my Aunt Nina's house—it's in the middle of nowhere. The media will have a hard time tracking me down there.'

His hand shot further out, blocking her from leaving the room. 'Hold on. Why would you go and stay with your aunt?'

Remain dignified. Don't cry, don't plead. Don't think you can change his mind. Don't do any of the things that stripped Dad of his pride and self-worth.

'You can say I'm ill…or whatever excuse you want to use for me not attending the enthronement. I'm guessing there's nothing your father can do once you've acceded to the throne.'

Edwin stood squarely in front of her. Pale and horrified. 'You're leaving?'

She winced at the distress in his whisper, her threatening tears turning to ones of pure confusion and anger. 'Isn't that what you want?'

He stepped back, and then strode into the room, raking a hand through his hair. 'Of course I don't want you to leave. *Dio*, Kara!' His voice was rising all of the time, his horror replaced by dismay. 'I have told you time and time again that I would never want to separate from you. Why won't you believe me?'

'Why won't I believe you? Oh, give me a break, Edwin. We both know you're only in this marriage to succeed to the throne.' She threw her hands up into the air.

Stop it. You said you wanted to leave with dignity.

Well, I don't care now. I want to lash out. I want to be angry. I'm so fed up with pretending and being nice. I'm too upset and heartbroken to shut up.

'We both know it makes you deeply uncomfortable—we barely speak, you can't bear to look at me and at night you turn your back on me.'

Turning away, she ran into their bedroom and then into her dressing room next to it. She flung back the sliding door of the wardrobe where her weekend bag was stored, wincing at the sight of her wedding dress, which was being stored there temporarily. The national museum wanted it for a special display to celebrate their wedding. They wouldn't now.

'It's not the marriage that's the problem, it's me.'

The bitterest, most cynical laugh she had ever made erupted from deep inside of her. She whirled around to face him. 'Oh, please—not the *It's not you, it's me* line.'

Why was he looking so upset? He had no right to be. She grabbed some T-shirts and bundled them into her weekend bag, burning humiliation torching her skin. She was failing everyone. Failing the charity. Failing Michael's memory. Failing all of the people who relied on the charity. Failing everyone who had come to their wedding in good faith.

'I never wanted to fall in love with you.'

Her hand stalled where she had grabbed a pile of underwear. The white, pastel, bright red and pink colours of her underwear blurred together. He had never seen her wear any of them. How many wives could say that of their husband? She closed her eyes. Pushed down on the hope that stirred somewhere deep in her stomach, disappointment making her feel faint and nauseous. She placed a hand on the frame of the wardrobe to steady herself, reality and memories forti-fying her. 'I'm sorry to tell you that I'm well versed in *I love you* being used as a get-out-of-jail-free card. It was a speciality of Nick's any time I tried to break up with him. He would suddenly transform from being indifferently cruel to being the most loving and thoughtful boyfriend a girl could wish for. He was a master of manipulation. What had you expected, that you would waltz in here this morning and we would have a nice little chat about being honest and I would just say okay and agree to staying in a marriage that was destroying me?'

White noise crowded his head. Panic crawled beneath his skin. Why did it physically hurt so much to talk, to express everything that was swarming inside of him?

Making an angry sound, Kara hurled some underwear into her suitcase, the light cotton landing like confetti. Then, yanking at her hand, she shoved her engagement ring towards him. 'Here.'

Dio! She really was serious about leaving.

'No…it's yours.'

The brilliance of the blue stone caught in the sharp light of the recessed lighting. He had spent hours working with Alberto Enciso, the head designer at the royal jewellers, Frechilla &

Rouet, designing the ring and picking the exact shade of stone to match Kara's eyes.

'It will never belong to anyone else.'

Her mouth tightened, her eyes blazed with disdain. 'Oh, yeah, I'd forgotten that it would never be part of the royal collection. A fake ring for a fake marriage.'

'It's an eight-carat sapphire! There's nothing fake about it.'

Her nose wrinkled, her mouth twisted. 'That's not what I meant. My point is it's not from the royal collection.'

Lost, he stared down at the ring she was still thrusting towards him. Her hand was shaking, her fingertips white where she was grasping the ring. He had thought his choice of ring would symbolise to Kara his desire to create something unique just for her. Instead she had clearly seen it as a form of rebuttal. *Dio*, he had got so many things wrong. 'Why did you refuse to wear jewellery from the royal collection?'

Her nose wrinkled even more, her cheeks grew hot. 'Because I thought you wouldn't want me to.'

Aghast, he leant against the door frame, ran a hand against the screaming tightness in his temples. 'You don't believe that I see you as part of this family now, do you?' It was as much a question to her as a realisation to him.

Her bottom lip trembled for a split second before she whipped around and tugged open another drawer in her wardrobe. This time, sweaters in her favourite colours of cobalt blue, bright red and pure black hit the suitcase.

He was so tired of living a lie. Tired of being terrified of losing her. So tired of being terrified by emotional intimacy because of the potential pain of growing close to a person and losing them. So tired of closing his heart, of hiding himself from her in fear of appearing foolish, of failing in his promise to protect her.

He opened his mouth, a hot sensation running through his body. 'I have things I need to say to you,' he paused, lost for words, 'things about me and my life I've never shared with you before. Or with anyone else.' He gave a mirthless laugh. 'You see, that's the problem—there hasn't really been anyone else in my life except you for the past decade. You have been the star around which my life has revolved.'

She turned with a sneer, folding her arms.

She wasn't buying it. And he couldn't blame her. Not after Nick's games. And especially given just how closed he had been with her throughout their friendship and especially since they had made love.

He ran a hand through his hair, frustrated and scared he was going to get this wrong. 'I swear

I'm not trying to manipulate you. I've been living a lie for so long, and I'm tired of it.'

She made an impatient sound before brushing past him. Out in the bedroom she pulled back the curtains to the early morning sky and went and sat on the sofa in the sitting area. She crossed one leg over the other, her dressing gown parting to reveal her thigh. Seeing his gaze, she tugged the material back in place. Folded her arms and waited for him to speak with a cynical eyebrow raised.

He sat beside her but after a few seconds stood again, needing to move.

He paced the room, his shoulders on fire from tension. He rolled them but found no relief. His skin burnt. He came to a stop, forcing himself to sit and talk to her at the same level, eye to eye, even though he felt sick with the thought of having to open himself up to her. 'I'm in love with you. Not as a friend. As your husband.'

She winced. 'Why should I believe you?'

He glanced at their bed, his chest tightening. 'The night we made love…' He paused, the horror, the slamming disappointment of her words the following morning, coming back to him. He cleared his throat. 'I thought we spoke then, not in words but in our lovemaking. But the day after, you said it was a mistake.'

Kara shifted forward in her seat, her arms dropping to her sides. Stared at him.

Dio, she had seen his tears.

He wanted the ground to swallow him up.

'Edwin.' She said his name as a sigh. She ran a hand down her cheek, closing her eyes for long moments before opening them again. 'It *was* a mistake because it shifted my love for you from being a friend to being your wife.' She sighed deeply, shook her head. 'I don't know why I'm saying these things, but I get it when you say you're tired of lying. So am I.'

What was she saying? Was she saying she was in love with him? He worked his jaw, the adrenaline of panic sending his pulse into a frenzy. He opened his mouth, closed it again.

Dammit, just ask her.

'Are you saying you love me?'

Her hand, trembling, moved against her mouth, her cheeks flaming. 'I'm in love with you…' his heart soared, but crashed to the floor at the pain etched in her eyes '…but I can't stay in this marriage.'

'Why…if you love me and I love you?'

'But they're just words. I love you, Edwin. I love your honour, your sense of duty, your drive to do the best for your country, your inherent decency. But I'm lonely. I'm lonelier in our marriage than I have ever been in my entire life. You feel so distant from me.' A large tear dropped along her cheek, and she gave an unhappy laugh. 'I swore I wouldn't do this. I can't live in a marriage where I don't feel safe, and I don't feel safe with you because you shut me out.'

Her words cut him in two, their honesty searing his heart. His throat was on fire. It felt like a monumental task to even open his mouth to speak. Years of silence and denial had made him psychologically mute. But he *had* to speak. Or else he was going to lose her. 'I'm terrified of losing you, but the crazy thing is I shut you out because I'm scared of the pain that would come if I did lose you—it's this crazy circle of avoidance that feeds itself and it's out of control.'

Her hand trailed over the soft lace edges of her dressing gown. 'You won't lose me.'

He smiled at that. 'You were just packing your bags.'

She gave a guilty smile. 'I was running away, embarrassed by my feelings for you. I wasn't really thinking, but deep down I was hoping we'd stay friends...that maybe with time and a small miracle we'd be able to go back to where we were.'

He held her gaze. The blue-eyed gaze that had spat fire all those years ago when he had plucked her off a muddy pitch. 'I don't want to be your friend. I want to be your husband. And not just in name.'

Such beautiful words. Words that could turn a world upside down. But meaningless if they weren't backed up by action and truth and real connection. Her parents' marriage had been destroyed by a lack of truth and connection.

If their marriage had any hope of surviving then they both needed to speak the truth, expose what was really in their hearts. She felt faint and, no matter how hard she tried to breathe in, she wasn't capable of dragging in enough air to feed the panic pushing her heart to near exploding point. 'I'm in love with you, but relationships, marriage, terrify me.' She wanted to stop but knew she needed to continue and blurted out without drawing breath, 'Losing Michael, my parents' marriage imploding, my relationship with Nick have all made me wary of trusting that people will be there, will be truthful and honest with me. And so far in our marriage it doesn't feel like we've had any of that.'

Grimacing, Edwin shifted his gaze away from her. He bowed his head. Studied his clasped hands. A long silence followed. Her heart raged in her chest. He was doing it again, closing down on her. She wanted to weep with frustration. He had spoken his oath to her, saying he wanted to be honest with her. And yet he kept shutting her out, as though he didn't trust himself, or simply want, to fully open his heart to her.

'I learned at a very young age that I have to present a mask to the world. When my mother died I was scared and angry, I wanted to rebel, to walk away from everything. But how could I? I was the heir to the throne, the oldest son. I *had* to be responsible. I had to be the one who remained in control while Luis went crazy and Ivo went silent.' He clasped and unclasped his hands, tension radiating from him. 'And the mask I had learned to pull on when in public soon became a private mask too.' He cleared his throat and stared unseeingly at a point beyond her shoulder. 'I used to think I could hear her footsteps outside my bedroom door. I was certain I caught glimpses of her walking around corners of the palace. I thought I was going crazy. I felt so weak. I could barely function. Princess Maria tried to help me, but I couldn't bear to talk. I was afraid that if I did start talking everything I was holding in would spiral out of control.'

Her heart broke to hear his bewildered pain. He looked at her and inhaled a long, deep breath full of remorse. 'With Michael, I should have helped him. I should have been a better friend but I was so closed to my own emotions I just panicked. I didn't know how to help him.'

A tight band squeezed her chest. 'You did help. You spoke to the university authorities and my parents.'

He shrugged away her comment.

Her stomach churned and her throat was raw. She dug her nails into the palms of her hands.

Ask him! For God's sake, ask him!

'Was it because of Michael that you stayed friends with me?'

Those golden eyes burnt into hers. 'No, you had already got under my skin.'

Her heart tumbled, emotion clogged her throat. She dipped her head to meet his gaze and whispered, 'We all feel guilt. We all wish we could have done more for him. I don't think that regret will ever leave us.' She paused, struggling to find the right words. 'You haven't been the only one hiding. I have too. I've been hiding even from myself.'

His hand reached out to rest on the cushion between them. 'What do you mean?'

'For far too long I've been too terrified to accept my feelings for you because I thought it would destroy our friendship. I was too proud to be honest about my feelings because I never wanted to be humiliated. I guess I need to learn from that. And the best way we can honour Michael is by trying to lead truthful lives ourselves, where we don't hide our pain.'

'Losing my mother, witnessing Ivo's pain, the way my family has floundered ever since… shutting down was the easiest way to cope.'

She nodded in understanding. 'Before our engagement, I thought I was okay with the fact that you were so private and closed off. It suited me that we had distance between us. But being married, being around you all of the time, the intimacy of it all, that distance went from being okay to just being very alone and uncertain and insecure.'

He shifted closer to her, those golden eyes searing into hers. He was only inches away from her, both of their heads bowed as though in confession. 'Do you believe me when I say I love you?'

'I don't know… It's so strange to hear you saying you love me after all these years,' she whispered back.

He moved even closer, his mouth close to her ear. 'But it feels completely natural for me to say it. I love you. I love you, Kara Duffy, with your sexy laugh and glittering blue eyes. I love that you always try to beat me to the peak of every mountain we climb. I love your chatter all the way up and down that mountain. I love you for your optimism and humour and imagination. I love that you treat me like a normal human being, never pandering to me.'

She tilted her head, dizzy with the intimacy of his whispers, dizzy with the desire to believe him.

His hand touched against the silk material covering her leg. She pulled away from him, doubts suddenly crowding in.

He moved back towards her, a quiet determination in his eyes. 'When we slept together, it was the most right and real night of my life.' His voice was low, tender. She wanted to weep in relief. 'There was a truthfulness and honesty there that I desperately wanted to ignore, desperately wanted to pretend I didn't crave. That's why, despite it feeling like a kick in the teeth, I tried to pretend to myself that I agreed with you that it was all a mistake, when in fact it felt like the best thing that would ever happen in my life.'

'Are you really saying all of this because you love me—or is it due to the enthronement?'

He studied her with a quiet determination. 'I won't succeed to the throne in order to prove to you my love. Princess Maria can succeed instead.'

She leapt out of her chair, her mouth working

like a goldfish's before she finally managed to spit out, 'You're kidding me. You're not about to give up the throne, the role you were born for.'

Edwin shrugged, his expression deadly serious. 'I want you in my life. I want to be your husband. I want to spend every single day proving to you just how much I love you.' His voice cracked. Pinched lines appeared at the corners of his eyes. 'I will walk away from the crown to prove that to you.' Taking his phone from his pocket, he added, 'I can call my father now and tell him of my decision.'

'No!' She took the phone from him, threw it onto their bed. Faced him and said in low voice, 'You do love me.' She whispered those words as much for herself as him. Needing to hear the most amazing realisation of her life out loud.

His expression transformed into gentle delight and tenderness.

She blinked and said, 'Love is pretty terrifying, isn't it?'

'Yes, that's why I think we should ease into this.'

'What do you mean?' she asked.

'We skipped a whole lot of important stuff, like date nights.'

She eyed him. 'We've known each other for more than a decade.'

He took her hand. 'A decade where I've been

trying to deny my feelings for you. I've stood on the sidelines and watched you become this incredible woman with endless passion and empathy. A woman I hugely admire. A woman who makes every day worthwhile.'

Her heart about to beat its way out of her chest, she softly whispered, 'I love you. And I want to be your consort.'

Leading her to their bed, kicking off his shoes, he lay down on the mattress and opened his arms to her. She placed her head against his chest, his hand stroked her hair, and he told her a story of a misguided prince, too scared to love his wife until he found the courage to let her into his heart.

And later that day she stood at his side when he was crowned Sovereign Prince of Monrosa, her heart overflowing with pride and love.

EPILOGUE

GABRIELA'S TINY NOSE WRINKLED. She let out a mewl of protest as the cold holy water trickled down her forehead. But she immediately settled back into her deep sleep the moment Edwin drew her against his chest, a small smile lifting on her pink Cupid lips.

Kara reached out, laid a finger against her daughter's cheek. How could skin be so soft, so perfect? She shared a look with Edwin, the wonder in his eyes matching her own amazement. After three long years they finally had their much longed-for baby. At times, she had thought it would never happen for them, her arms aching with the need to hold Edwin's baby.

The cardinal blessed Gabriela and walked away towards the main altar of the palace's private chapel. Handing Gabriela to her godfather, Ivo, who studied his niece with intense pride and adoration, Edwin took her hand and lead her towards the altar too.

Confused, she turned and looked behind to their families. But they were following behind them. Her mother and father walking side by side, their annual trips to visit her in Monrosa for Christmas and during the summer helping to heal the wounds between all three of them. And now they were united in their adulation for their firstborn grandchild. In front of them, Edwin's father seemed to be swallowing back tears. He too knew just how desperately they had wanted Gabriela. Retirement hadn't suited him, but now that Edwin had convinced him to be the island's environmental ambassador he was thriving in his new role.

Edwin brought her to stand before the cardinal.

Touching his hand to her cheek, he said quietly, 'I thought this would be a good time to renew our vows.'

Really? She still looked pregnant, her boobs were sore and she sobbed at the drop of a hat. She eyed her husband, her rock, her life, her calm reassurance when yet another blue line would fail to appear, and nodded *yes*.

He smiled, his eyes pulling her into that private, intimate space they disappeared to when alone.

Then, handing her a white card, his looping handwriting on one side, he said, 'I thought I should write our vows this time.'

At the cardinal's invitation he spoke his vows first. Not once did he look down at the card. Not once did he falter in his delivery. He knew the words as though they were etched onto his brain.

When it was her turn, she laughed when Edwin handed her a clean handkerchief embroidered with his initials—he knew her so well—and, swiping away her tears, through a voice choked with love and hope, she spoke the words her husband had written for them both. 'You are my best friend, my ally, my safe harbour in life. I promise to give you my trust and honesty, my truthful love. I promise to take risks for you. I promise to be always there for you. You are my heart. Dance and laugh and love with me for ever.'

* * * * *